Advance Praise

Syr Hayati Beker's transformed and transformative fairy tales are like nothing else you have ever read. Lyrical, resonant, weirdly wonderful, wildly inventive.

— Karen Joy Fowler, the *New York Times* bestselling author of *The Jane Austen Book Club*, *We Are All Completely Beside Ourselves*, and *Booth*

What to say about Syr Hayati Beker's *What a Fish Looks Like*: maybe that it deconstructs and reassembles the fairy tale; maybe that it is a most imaginative speculation; maybe that it is a wholly original and pulsing love story, of so many iterations of love. Or maybe that love cannot be iterative because love is the vine, the snow, the material of it all. Maybe you will stare at the ocean after you read it. Maybe you will feel the ocean churn in your gut. A host of maybes, because this book is an homage to the word. But what is certain: Beker wrote it with so much dazzling spirit you are going to burst. This book lit me alive.

— Miah Jeffra, Author of *American Gospel* and *The Fabulous Ekphrastic Fantastic!* Co-Founder of Foglifter Journal & Press

From the dedication to the last word, this book is unexpected and brilliant — a deeply queer and riotously joyful lament for our world, so wildly creative, original, and unrestrained it makes the care and artistry with which it's been weaved seem effortless. *What a Fish Looks Like* is one of the most special and memorable books I have ever read.

— Natalia Theodoridou, Nebula and World Fantasy Award winning author of *Sour Cherry*

What a Fish Looks Like is a phantasmagoric read. Inventive and playful with form, Syr Hayati Beker fuses horror, science fiction, and magic to inspire, subvert, and expand our understanding of family, gender identity, and sexuality. In retelling and repositioning these fairy tales in contemporary times, Beker's stories exist to remind us that love is a necessary and courageous choice, not something or someone to be found.

— Ploi Pirapokin, author of *The Greenest Gecko*

Kaleidoscopic and fearlessly innovative, *What a Fish Looks Like* shatters the boundaries of climate fiction. It's a fierce, tender testament to the power of love, memory, and chosen community in the face of collapse. The book invents a new language for what it feels like to grieve a dying world, and to imagine something radically different in its place.

— Kate Folk, author of *Sky Daddy* and *Out There*

What a Fish Looks Like is a virtuoso performance, a huge-hearted, wildly inventive collection of interlinked stories about queers falling in and out of love with the world and each other as they debate whether love is enough reason to stay. Beker's joyous formal play sharpens their compassionate insight into how people survive an earth beset by endings — exploitation, extinction, that ex you can't forget. This book is a talisman: keep it with you, for the apocalypse and everything after.

—B. Pladek, author of *Dry Land*

A beautiful, strange, moving and haunting book. Syr Hayati Beker is a rare and visionary talent.

— Steven Hall, author of *The Raw Shark Texts* and *Maxwell's Demon*

In a soaring tribute to friends, to chosen family, to community, to the beloved places we call home — and ultimately, to queer love and survival — Syr Hayati Beker's *What A Fish Looks Like* transports readers to a near future where climate change has rendered our planet unrecognizable. When all our favorite places have been swallowed by the sea, burned in a blaze, or claimed by poisonous vines, do we say goodbye to Earth, or do we stay and try to build something beautiful from the detritus? This is not a simple question, and *What A Fish Looks Like* does not present simple solutions — just humans grappling with the complex — and often heartbreaking — consequences of either decision. This novel-in-fairytales made me want to hold my loved ones tight. I wept.

— Lauren C. Johnson, author of *The West Façade* and co-founder of Club Chicxulub

Inventive, delightful, heartbreaking. Set in an ecosystem on its last breath, this book will make you want to run to the nearest ocean or forest; will make you want to eat leaves and touch the face of everyone you've ever loved. Simply brilliant.

— Nona Caspers, author of *The Fifth Woman*

What a Fish Looks Like is wild, electric, necessary writing. These linked stories and ephemera recast known tales with spellbinding new inclusions during climate collapse. With refreshingly human characters in their pettiness, vulnerability, and love, plus fluidity and grief, these are innovative stories we need now and in the future.

— Heidi Kasa, author of *Split*, and *The Bullet Takes Forever*

From the belly of the wolf to the bottom of the sea, Syr Hayati Beker's profound *What a Fish Looks Like* rewrites the world on the bones of fairy tales. With a deft, light touch, Beker reveals a near-future Bay Area sliding towards a specific form of uninhabitable — the vines, the cats, the hot, hot oceans — and peoples it with humans that honor how, in the face of anything, we continue to be interested and interesting. We adapt and adapt and adapt; even as air becomes unbreathable, individual heartbreak and acceptance matters. As characters unfurl on scaffolds of literature, from Greek tragedy to text messages, *What a Fish Looks Like* does the difficult work of holding beautiful and aching contradictions. Beker tells us that, "Theatre is what you do when crying isn't enough," and they have brought us a book that offers just such depth and solace and possibility. It is a map that lines ways through the woods of our impending futures. Like all great books, *What a Fish Looks Like* is a map of love. You should read it. I'm so glad I did.

— Kathryn Kruse, author of *To Receive My Services You Must Be Dying and Alone*

A queer-as-hell mending kit for a threadbare world.

— T.K. Rex, author of *The Wildcraft Drones*

What a Fish Looks Like

What a Fish Looks Like

Cover art by Carly A-F
https://carlydraws.carrd.co/

Interior section illustrations by Zeph Fishlyn
https://www.zephrocious.com/

Interior design by Selena Middleton

Edited by Selena Middleton

Published by Stelliform Press
Hamilton, Ontario, Canada
https://stelliform.press

Library and Archives Canada Cataloguing in Publication
Title: What a fish looks like / Syr Hayati Beker.
Names: Beker, Syr Hayati, author. Identifiers: Canadiana (print) 20250207982 | Canadiana (ebook) 20250211270 | ISBN 9781738316557 (softcover) | ISBN 9781738316564 (EPUB)
Subjects: LCGFT: Novels.
Classification: LCC PS3602.E42 W43 2025 | DDC 813/.6—dc23

À Kadet
… peu m'importe
si tu m'aimes

What a Fish Looks Like

Syr Hayati Beker

Stelliform Press
Hamilton, Ontario

Dear Seb,

I am leaving you this book of fairy tales you loved so much.

I don't understand what use you have for it, now that there are no more woods, no oceans, no wetlands, no frogs left to kiss, at least none that won't keep disappointing you.

Whatever you were endlessly looking for in these stories, whatever made them so important to you, I hope you find it.

Take care,

Jay

The Collected
Fairy Tales
Stories of Wonder
& Bravery

This Book Belongs To:

____

~~The Gorgeous Fifth Extinction, BB!~~

~~BuiltIn Obsolescence~~

~~The Public Library of Uranus~~

~~Paradise DeVine~~

~~The Fungal Mentalists~~
~~Doomsday Collective~~

~~KC, Drunk at The Paradise, found this book.~~

~~Everyone~~

~~Octavia's Collective~~
~~RIP Octavia's Collective~~

~~Nowhere Collective~~
~~Jay & Seb, in love at the end of the world.~~

Seb. Alone.
World's still here though.☺

INVITATION

Party @ Paradise Bar

Thursday. Sunset. Celebrating
Galactic Exodus 3, T-minus 10.

BYOB IF YOU CAN. | TELL EVERYONE.

SEB!!! Party. At. The. Paradise. Tonight!
It's behind No Exit Theater.
In case you forgot where outside is.
You're not sitting around with your books.
It's like 70 days before Exodus 3!
Jay's whole little group — Now Collective —
they're probably all getting on that ship. Nerds.
Your ex is going to Space!
Let's dance about it!
xoxoxxx
Dion

Not going. — Seb

Introduction to this Collection

With Notes by Seb

"Once upon a time …" so begins the classic fairy tale …
Fine. I'll play. Once upon a time there was a city at the edge of a dying ocean. In this city, two people locked eyes across the ruins of a building, and fell in love.

Their origin shrouded in mystery, they endure …
They lived together through floods and storms and droughts. They built a community and called it Nowhere. They said: at least we have each other. When the world ends, we'll be holding hands.

from the first hint of magic
But the world didn't end. It just kept on, crumbling streets, silent water, heavy air.

… to the happily ever after.
Until one of them (you, Jay) left me. And my world ended.

Fairy Tales have existed for as long as there have been woods.
Imagine so many trees you can get lost in them. If you can't, imagine two people clinging to one another on a rooftop under an orange sky, arguing about whether to keep things like this book, or fundraising stickers with a black and white bear, when both the fund and bear are long gone.

They will continue to exist for as long as there are fish in the sea.

A fish, dear reader-who-may-never-exist, was a gill-bearing animal that lived in the ocean. See the drawings at the back.

And as long as there are storytellers, like the brothers Grimm and Andrew Lang

Fairy tales are the project of colonialism, you'd say. Take Andrew Lang, extracting stories from across the empire. He didn't even write those books, his wife did. The Grimms were gentrifiers. What did these stories ever teach us but to follow the damn path?

But then you sat next to me on that rooftop, leaning your bony elbows into me, and we told stories. We imagined the sky blue and the crumbling streets covered in wildflowers. And I took the birds from the stories in this book, nightingales and phoenixes and robins, and painted them into the ruins outside because of how you listened.

who made it their life's work to preserve stories.

There is no going back, you said. Why bother remembering? I never could give you a reason, except that in these pages, in these stories, there used to be woods.

The stories survive …

Only this page survives. The rest is a mess of overwriting, sun bleaching, swollen pages dropped in water, dragged across the ground, rings from your tea mugs, blood from the time you climbed down into the sinkhole because you thought someone might be in there, and all I could do was wait and cry.

… in the tradition of Lang's Rainbow Fairy Tale books, we present this edition …

What should we call this one then? The Bleached Coral White edition? The Silent Spring Orange book? The Green Invasion, for the vines crawling all over our buildings, and their overactive pollen that makes it hard to breathe? Or maybe just the Seb Alone Edition.

Of course these are retellings of retellings.
The stories are changing, like the tales I tell myself about us and who we were, like our city, becoming stranger and harder to live in every day.

… but they have this in common, a sense of wonder beyond our world
Which brings me to my point, dear reader-who-may-never-exist. They found a planet, not too far away, very much like our own used to be. They say it has plant matter, breathable air, maybe even a mountain to climb. If we hurry, we could reach it before it orbits away.

For as we huddle at the edge of the woods
Galactic Exodus 3, final ship, leaves in 10 days with room for 2,700 on board. Last week, 100 tickets surfaced in our community. No one knows how. Rumor says Ali of B. Collective showed up with them one day, holding them up to show their watermarks and numerical codes. Dion says they were found in a dark alley near human remains, even the bag had teeth marks. Maybe there weren't enough people who wanted them. Even now, it's hard to imagine leaving Earth behind.

We tell one another stories
The point is that by next week, half of our community will be gone forever. And because I know you, Jay-as-in-Jetpack of Now Collective, I already know what you're going to do.

to understand the world

In ten days, you will be on that spaceship with my memories, and the stories I told you, and the nightingales I gave you, and the moments we shared that exist nowhere else.

We tell them differently every time.
All I have are these barely readable pages, and you, that's all I have. And that's why I can't let you go.

~~These~~ **are the stories that** ~~survive.~~
We   are still here.

Table of Contents

The stories are changing, like everything else.
They are starting to look like us.

FULL COLOR ILLUSTRATIONS

1. ~~In an underwater cave, The Little Mermaid gazes at a sunken statue of the young prince.~~ **Bathroom door at The Paradise,** drawn by Maxxy

2. ~~A Little Match Girl Sees a Vision Of Love~~ **A Memorial,** recorded by Maxxy.

3. ~~Red Riding Hood Speaks to the Wolf; Two Paths Lay Before Her~~ **Inauguration of New Paradise,** recorded by Maxxy

Seb. SEB!
The hell did I just see?
Was that actually you at
The Paradise dancing with
Jay? JAY?
If you get this, come tell
me everything. Back in a
few, after DESSERT.
xoxxx

Dion

Ps: Got an Exodus 3
ticket. I'll probably sell it
later.

I. ~~Tales of Enchanted Animals~~
Tales of the Post Extinction

Letter from Seb at Here Collective
to Jay at Now Collective

Dear Jay-as-in-Jetpack,

I've taken the liberty of placing this book in your backpack.

It was nice kissing you tonight. You've barely changed since you took half our friends and made a whole new collective. How are all your future-minded friends? Has Science come to rescue you yet?

Incidentally and wholly out of curiosity, have you made a decision about Exodus 3?

Because being this close to takeoff made me think of 3 years ago at The Paradise, when you said we'd always have one another to dance with until the sky fell. I believe those were your exact words.

I've been re-reading that story you loved so much, about a woman who falls in love with a beast who then becomes human, like love is some great improvement project. I wonder if that's what you thought would happen with me.

We definitely loved this planet to death.

Do you think it's right to leave something just because it doesn't live up to your expectations?

I'm speaking exclusively of Earth here, of course.

Enjoy the book. Whoever you're wrapping yourself around this week, maybe they could read you one last story.

Yours,

Saint Sebastian Full of Arrows

PS: Have you seen Dion?

~~Beauty and the Beast~~
What a Fish Looks Like

My Grandmother knit the Ocean.

Up all night with bargain-basement yarn, she watched her old nature shows and knitted fish. Silver fish, red fish, pink-and-orange-polka-dot-vodka fish. She finished each with a knot and prayer-spit and set it out to sea, which was her room in my mother's house, painted blue. She knit fish like it was her job to fill the ocean, then she switched needles and made coral reef, filling the space with soft fractals, every color but white.

Habibti, she would say, a clownfish between her fingers, and another word I can't remember that in my dreams brings all the fishes back to life.

My grandma died and then the ocean died. Both left blue rooms, one full, one empty.

And so last month, when you packed your boots, your flashlight, and a belt that was definitely mine into a box, there was no one to tell me, *There are plenty of fish in the sea.* Which is to say that after you said, "I don't think this is working, I mean us, I mean this," waving at the walls you insisted we paint yellow, I searched for words to keep me from unraveling and found none.

And because you never got to meet my grandmother, you probably think the reason I chose to *ghost* was because of you. Just to be clear: 1) there is absolutely nothing reckless about my decision; and 2) it had nothing to do with you.

Ghosting used to mean not answering someone's calls and texts. Now it means you go to one of those special labs that have appeared in our cities. I went to the one near our coffee shop, the Expresso, where you first reached for my hand. In the past, ghosting would have meant avoiding the Expresso, our street, and all the places we used to go. Now, it's the word we use to refer to the decision a small number of people have made. *Ghosting* means I open a reflective door and find myself in a sterile room where a woman with perfect bangs hands me a form and a pen, and tells me to take my time with the answers.

I sit down next to a guy about my age, with lighter brown skin and bleached spiky hair. One of his sneakers squeaks and his pants are too low. Evidence: three hairs emerging like dandelions from the front of his concrete-gray jeans.

Now, when you tell people I *ghosted*, they'll picture me here, filling out a form in a lab close to our apartment, initials on every page, while this boy, Dandelion, tries to get a word in.

"Don't worry about it too much," he says, "I don't think they actually read it." He laughs a bit too long.

The ghosting form begins with a space for my legal name and the official name of the procedure — Voluntary DNA Surrogacy — both of which are obsolete. I skip through two pages of explanations and cautions, to the part of the form that wants me to think about what I would be giving up.

Do you accept the terms and conditions of the procedure?

["Do you think we'll ever see a dolphin again?"
you asked at the Expresso, a million years ago,
and I was going to answer but you paused,
shifted, and leaned against me. I smiled and gave
you my drink to finish, and then the electricity
went out like it does all the time in fire season,
and we went back to my apartment, and you
knocked over a glass, and you laughed and
apologized because back then you didn't know
everything I had was yours.]

Yes, I write. Initials.

Do you understand that the procedure is permanent and irreversible?

[The first people to ghost were told the infusion
would be temporary, that they would only be
lending their body for a short amount of time.
A year. Or five. Ten at the most.]

Yes. I understand that the procedure is perma-
nent, which is different than "forever," which
means nothing at all.

Sex:

["Clownfish," I said. "Began as males and
became females. Kobudai did the opposite.
Gobies switched all the time. Now they're
gone." "We're still here," you said, and smiled,
and I clung hard to that "we."]

F, is the box I check, options being limited.

Emergency Contact:

> ["You know what your problem is?" you said,
> tired of all the nights I spent at work, at the lab,
> listening to ocean water instead of with you,
> "Your problem is …"]

> I hesitate, and finally write your name.

Species Preference:

> I pause over this last question. Dandelion
> watches me pause.

> I'd prefer to be invulnerable. I want claws and
> jaws and height. I want there to be a box with
> my name on it, and when I check it, I want the
> power grid to surge and for every room to be
> flooded with light.

> ["… your problem is you don't know when to let
> go."]

Species Preference:

> I write, None. No preference.

And I stand up to take the form to the desk before I can change
my mind, pen clattering to the floor.

⚓

When we were together, we would tell one another our own heroic stories about how it was all worth it; your actions, my research.

"In the future, they build monuments to protestors, plant a tree for your friends who were hurt, or killed, or arrested. The city is covered in green, even the sidewalks will breathe."

"The ocean is full of fish. There's a boat named after you. A crew of sailors rows out to open waters. They throw fish back in, by the netful, so many fish you could walk across the surface of the ocean and never get wet."

We laughed and coughed on the smoke and checked our window seals.

"Anyone can live in Utopia. We get to be part of making it."

And the word *making* made me think of my grandmother, her reefs spreading across the floor, and a lost word to make it all live.

❧

After filling out forms, Dandelion and I are shown an informational video about ghosting.

Words scroll across the screen: hope, DNA, hereditary material, extinct species, the gratitude of future humanity. A white girl runs through a cornfield; a digitally-rendered shark swims and glitches; in a field that is a green I have never seen, it is raining from the sky; a sunrise, and pouring over the horizon, long shadows, suggesting the triumphant return of large extinct animals that must have been out of budget, at least for this film, at least for us.

After the inspirational music fades out, Dandelion picks up a magazine about furniture and puts it back down. I know he's going to talk to me long before he opens his mouth.

Him: What made you want to ghost?

Me: Oh, you know. The usual.

[Loss of you. Lost night after night at the lab, listening for the sounds that should have been the ocean and hearing none. Loss of you coming home lit up from a protest, sweaty and hopeful. Lost plankton, just a few drifting shells where there used to be an underwater galaxy.]

Him: Same.

[Like I hadn't noticed that his body was also missing a body: his sallow cheekbones, the lines under his eyes, the way his designer t-shirt draped where his belly should be.]

The rumor online in the forums — internet forums being all we have, since ghosting stopped being news — is that you need something for the ghost to take. It helps to have a recent absence, but we all know nothing-to-lose works too. A missing love, a missing cure, a billion missing white blood cells, or just a kind of reckless willingness. Any of these are good enough spaces for the ghost animals to come in and take residence until they can be set free, or passed on to the next (living) (human) carrier.

How you would have laughed at me for reading the forums. I bet Dandelion has read them. I could say something encouraging to him, but I don't.

They call his name first. He stands quickly, but then at the door he pauses, looks back at me. His eyes search for mine. I look away. This is the first time I feel something like fear, or the electricity right before you touch someone's hand for the first time, as if accidentally. The door to the street is open. The door to the back office will open soon. I check my phone's blue screen. Empty.

This is how science says ghosting works: DNA, blah, retro-something, blah, mapping whatsit, splicing something, CRISPR-for-your-pleasure, preservation of extinct species, infusing extinct animal DNA within living carriers, look at all my syllables.

In those early days, we laughed at headlines like "Hope for the Dodo: Could Humans Adopt Animal DNA?" Ghosting offices appeared, open for volunteers. It was a pharmaceutical solution, a practical solution. What do you do with extincting species? Inject them directly into your veins.

This is how ghosting actually works:

Step One: Imagine a box, cardboard. If you kick it, it moves around a little too much. It makes a sound like there's something inside. Science told us it would be simple, like a magic trick: in goes the DNA, out come fur, scale, and feather springing back to life in a few years, as soon as the world is ready again. No big deal. It's just DNA. It's not like humans would change.

So an ex-famous actor announced he would carry for Arctic fox. A pop singer you liked took on the Electric Eel, and no one thought it much of a sacrifice.

Step Two: Imagine that someone could wear the shape of that box. Picture a kid in a Halloween tiger mask, but the mask keeps talking after the kid is gone. Picture a fish flapping in an empty room.

Three weeks past the date when a small river in the Amazon was supposed to be cleaned up but wasn't, the eel singer was found suffocated. Rumors say she forgot to breathe on land, but everyone knows it was probably just regular drugs. A month later, the Arctic fox actor disappeared. Rumors say he ran off into the woods, where woods used to be. Most likely he just drifted out of public attention.

Those were the first trials. Science apologized. We forgave Science, like you won't forgive me. We gave Science another chance, even after it became clear that we didn't know what a successful DNA surrogacy — ghost — would look like, or how long it would take until we'd know how to bring the animals back, and what happens to people holding ghosts in the meantime.

Step Three: Now imagine that someone, someone like me, could hold the shape of the box inside their own. It's not like sharing a bed, struggling at first and then finding a rhythm. It's not like grafting an apricot branch to a plum tree. It is: your DNA turned into a factory for the DNA of extinct species until the day the world is safe enough that we can let the ghosts out, resurrected. Until then, it's a shorter life, but maybe less lonely. Maybe that's all there ever was.

Just a few months after the first big announcement, the hope of ghosting faded. There was no evidence that it worked. Why volunteer to carry an absence? As for the habitats, there was an adjustment of projections: five years became fifteen became twenty. Picture a fish, still swimming, looking for an escape, while the person around them gradually disappears. Why risk your life for a ghost animal that has nowhere to go?

Except the rumors remained. That somewhere out there, the ghost animals survived, that something of their animalness was tangible, so real it could almost be seen. That out there, somehow, extinct animals walked among us, treading paw prints down our streets, rippling once-still waters.

"How could it possibly work," you would ask me, "it's not like a telephone game, where you pass the message down. Gone is gone."

But you never saw my grandmother's room, a seahorse springing to life between her fingers, the way her coral reef carried the memory of the living ocean she swam in as a girl, the feeling that one day, it would all come back, a flood of life tearing the door off its hinges. And you never knew what it was to want something so much, like the ocean, like you, like that day at the Expresso when I asked you if you wanted to come home and you turned me incandescent with one single word.

The ghosting offices remained as though they had always been there. Everyone knew someone who knew someone who ghosted but no one could say, *Yeah, that was me.*

Now waiting for the door to open, I want to text you: *I'm doing it!* I could take my phone out right now and tell you. You could tell me to leave.

The door at the back of the office opens. I step through. In the silence of this last room, I think of sounds I have loved: needles and blue yarn, your feet on the stairs, an ocean wave — one as big as a house that obliterates the sun as it crests, and then turns the world upside down.

⁂

This is how ghosting actually feels: I wake up disoriented, hungry for fish, with a small hairball of consciousness that isn't mine. The part of me that once held you is mostly gone, replaced with a part of me that misses things I don't remember.

Like ice caps.

⁂

When I stumble back into the waiting room, I am surprised, then angry, then relieved to see Dandelion. He puts down his magazine and follows me outside. I suggest drinks because I don't know what else to do. He has the smoothest brow I have ever seen, even now. He snaps his fingers and hums. He beatboxes, ntz, ntz, ntz, like we're in Ibiza. He walks down the middle of *our* street and people get out of his way, and I hate him every step until we get to *our* bar and he takes out his wallet to pay.

When the bartender I've known for years looks at us, at our bandages, she smiles for the very first time and pours us all shots. When she turns away again, her shoulder blades are too pronounced, dark skin catching the light, threatening wings. I don't know why I never noticed.

Dandelion and I, we retreat to a table and try to talk about what it feels like.

"It's like I remember things, but they're not in words." [The feeling of ice under my]

"It's like I'm carrying something else inside me." He leans back in his chair, belly up. "I feel different," he says, "graceful." He basks in the light of the bar.

"I feel different," I say, "hungry." [My jaw hurts with wanting to close on something]

He is asking me a question, but behind him, snow is beginning to fall on the sticky oak bar, and there is a rift between two caps, and dark water.

I blink. Ask him to say that again.

"What did they give you?" He points at his bandage, at the vein spreading a new message across his body.

I look at my release form and the little paragraph about drinking water, meditating, a number you can call that has been disconnected for months, about what to expect, as if anyone can say. Most of the people who ghosted say they felt nothing at all, other than a week of confusion. The rest have gone silent, social media accounts inactive.

"Mine's Harp Seal," he says, making the words big, like he's announcing a new app:

"Harp Seal: Extinct 2027."

"Polar Bear, 2029" I read, to hide what shouldn't be a smile.

We both drink deep in the sudden awkwardness. Even years later, we remember how food chains work, and what polar bears eat.

I want to joke that they probably looked at me and thought I'd make a safer polar bear, but at the thought of having to explain it to him, to think about how I am seen in my body, to bring down on myself the shower of pink balloons and the lowering ceiling of his *gaze*, I find myself filled with the kind of rage that makes me a terrible choice for a polar bear. Outside, I smell the city that used to be there when you pulled my hand, laughing, down the street. I feel the outline of my body expanding — or maybe that's just what it's like to go without touch for so long. You grow a protective layer. You grow fur.

I tear into my cheap bar sushi.

Sealboy edges away. I fixate on his synthetic fish in the light of the bar with no snow.

If you believe the rumors, you know that four to six weeks is the time they say it takes for the ghost to take full possession. No one knows exactly why or what success looks like.

Four to six weeks into our relationship was enough for me to know I wanted you to move in. You told me about the house you shared with seventeen other activists and the single bathroom, the postcard parties, blocking bridges, closing down ports. I told you about my work listening to dead ocean water.

What are you looking for? you asked.

And when I couldn't answer, you put your hand on mine and said, I know you'll find it.

And I believed you.

But you're not here, and so I take a trip to the edge of town to see my grandmother's room. The door opens with one hard push, and there is her ocean in front of me.

In the real ocean, the coral reef is gone, but here in my grandmother's room, it's still there. It's not perfect, but you can stand in the doorway and squint and imagine how it was, a blue room with everything alive, everything shiny, every mouth open to brine.

A siren outside dissolves into the call of seagulls swooping, a cold wind, the splash of ink-blue water, snapping shrimp, whale song, a scattering school. A pufferfish makes patterns out of sand, a manta ray blocks the sun, seaweed sways and tangles like empty hangers in an old closet and then I am back in a room with blue peeling paint, waiting for DNA to resolve into a command my body won't be able to resist.

⁂

Five weeks in, and it feels like I'm trying to say something in a language I don't know.

In graduate school, the year they changed Marine Biology to Marine Paleontology, and when you asked me, "what are you looking for in those dead waters," and again when you said, "why can't you just come out and protest?" I would think of my grandmother's hands restoring a starfish, and search for words I could not remember or understand.

Some lines are extinct forever: language they didn't pass on to you, the last Kaua'i 'ō'ō bird singing for a mate, the absence of a person from your life, the melt of snow.

But some mornings now, I wake up and the air is cold on my tongue.

The word was —

Snow. Or maybe water. Or current.

⋘

Two months since the infusion, and this polar bear I am ghosting won't let me forget plastic, how it crowds your throat so you can't catch air, like the inflatable raft we brought to the lake, you and I, the lake we drove to in my car that was itself ghosting dinosaurs. We floated on the surface of the water in our plastic raft and almost drowned trying to kiss.

The bear won't let me forget glass, how it takes thousands of years to decompose, like the bottle of wine we drank on the rocky shore we imagined green again.

Polar bears don't mate for life and are not monogamous; they don't argue about the relative merits of memory or action, they don't even leave their compostable teabags in the sink; so the part of myself that won't forgive me is not the polar bear.

Our lake is mostly gone now, a few inches of sludge and weeds and the imprint of water, and if I could only remember it perfectly, enough to paint it all back, or if I could just remember the word, I might not be out here, looking for cold water in an endless empty summer.

The word was —
Thirsty.

⋘

These days, most days, I walk down the street, ghosting for polar bear.

It feels like stepping into a skin that extends far beyond me, all muscles and claws where I used to be soft. It never wants to rest, and neither do I. Bigger than me, this feeling of size.

Not yet, I think, but I lose myself in the way people step out of my path.

I walk the drifting sidewalks, snowy streets, walls that need no windows, only ice. I watch the wind that gathers snow and curls it softly against the sweet face of buildings.

I drag myself up so tall I can swipe at streetlights.

I drop from sidewalk to street and am surprised I can't immediately swim.

Between two ice floes, in a café, I see someone who looks like you and I fall hard back into small human shape.

I go home. I hold the last of my grandmother's fish with my fingers-becoming-claws. I remember the ocean, the way it really was, a blue room in which everyone belongs, maybe even me.

There was a time I thought you were right, that we could turn back the damage. One spring was not quite as hot. A farmer in Kansas saw a flock of birds. They found a frog that could burrow through wildfires. Scientists were biosynthesizing plankton. There was a day when the rain was safe enough, and people walked out of work with their faces turned up, and we kissed.

But then came the day we woke up to so much soot that the sky was orange and we could not see the sun. Birds died midair, murmurations in neat piles on the ground. Whole ecosystems folded like cardboard animals in a pop-up book, goodnight. Science, Government, and Tech withdrew their promises, one by one, just like you. Why did we believe them all along?

One night, you came home feverish from crowds, and chanting, and hope.

"Where were you?" you asked. "We need you out there."

I wanted you to explain it to me again, the breathing sidewalks, the trees, our lives meaning something. I envied the light in your face, you in church and me in a cold building without a door.

"What's the point of marching?"

"We can save it. You could join us."

"How? Explain to me how any of it can be saved. Explain to me why we get to save it."

You sat on the couch you insisted we rescue and closed your eyes. "Then what are you looking for in that water?"

A word in a language I don't know that brings all the fish back to life.

"Hell if I know," I said. I stormed out and back to the institute. I glared at the empty blue water. I listened to underwater recordings. Nothing.

But then I pulled a fraying fish out of my pocket and imagined the sounds that should have been there. I thought I heard the outline of something new: a giant shape-between-shapes, an absence larger-than-life, a waiting memory, like a tentacle curled around a rock.

On my way home, I saw someone walking out of a ghosting office, pausing for a second as if to say *what now*, but then turning and striding away purposefully, as if called.

Who goes there? I thought. *Who does that?* And then, *Why knit the ocean?*

Now, I close my eyes, I listen for my phone, water purling off my fur.

❧

Sealboy is starting to look good to me these days. We've been meeting for drinks. It's the new sleekness of his hips, his big shiny eyes, the fuzz on his rounding cheeks.

We're at the bar-where-you-can-also-dance. Around him, I try not to say the word *club*.

He holds his martini glass with his whole hand wrapped around the stem like a fin, and then spills it all over the bar. When he dances, he wriggles invitingly. I want to take him to the bathroom with the punk band posters plastered on the walls and lock the door and maul him.

"Wanna dance?" he asks, leaning close. His belly bumps mine.

"No, thank you," I say, as if waving off salmon.

There is a new patch of fur on the inside of my thigh. I check my phone.

⁂

When you finally text me back, it's hard to read.

Coffee next week?

My nails have grown so long, I can't retract them. I think of us; on the fire escape, on a rare clear night, searching the smoky sky for stars. It takes me a long time to text back *Yes*.

I try to get a beer, but my paws won't fit around the refrigerator handle.

Against the yellow kitchen wall, an outline of you.

"Enjoy your test tubes," you said that night, slamming the fridge door one last time.

"Enjoy your drum circles."

After you left, I watched live video of that action that put you in the news: the last elephant funeral. Two thousand people crying in public, in paper elephant masks. What's so hopeful about that?

I went for a walk and took a wrong turn. Instead of our café, there was a ghosting office. It must have always been there. I guess I never really saw it before.

⁂

In the week before seeing you, I love hard on a soft boy whose binder becomes a carapace. Black and red and shiny, it separates us, we separate.

"*Nicrophorus*," he apologizes.

I don't know the word.

"Beetle," he says. "Extinct 2028."

He moves to put on his shoes but then throws them into his bag instead. He doesn't need them anymore. The claws at the end of his articulated legs click the ground on his way out. I want to say goodbye, but my vocal cords are thickening. I envy him his exoskeleton. I envy him his willingness. I don't know where he is going, where they are all going, or who they will be when they get there, and I need to see you, if only to hear you say my name again, so I resist. I turn delicate brass knobs and stoop to walk through doorways correctly until I find the cloudy night sky and tilt my head back howling for want of snow.

☙

DNA isn't magic; it's just a sequence, a code. If DNA can unspool a memory of polar bear, then why isn't there a word that could restore the ocean, the rainforest, and any habitat, even ours?

The word is *jannah*, paradise or garden, which is what we thought we were creating, you painting blue whales in front of City Hall, and me at the lab, waiting for dead water to talk.

The word is my own name, how we spent a whole year reading through dictionaries to find it, only for you to spit it out months later with a comma and the word *goodbye*, linking them forever.

The word is *y'allah*, let's go, your extended hand, an invitation to come home.

☙

Now for the first time since you left, I push open the door to the café at the end of our street. The café that used to be ours is exactly the same: same round tables and mismatched chairs and same barista with the gemstone piercing and a name like Cakes or Muffin and an absolute refusal to smile.

The café that used to be ours is different: more menu items crossed off where the supply chain collapsed, a window pane broken and boarded up, and you are not at our table, but off to the side. I walk across the ice to you, paws gripping the linoleum.

We stop short of hugging and wave. You look exactly the way you did at the lake, your hair still wet from the shower, your cheeks red, the top three buttons on your flannel open, the freckle constellation under your collarbone. Stand up, I tell myself.

You tell me you're *great. Happy.* My spine wants to bend, my body drawn to the ground.

You tell me I look good. *Have I changed my hair?*

My shadow stretches up the wall behind you, up to the sky-light windows.

You tell me you're doing well, that the movement is going well. You're heading your own chapter now. There is a real chance you can save some wetlands. And you hope we can be friends. And you hope we can clear things up.

You always had so much hope.

"How's the research?" you ask. "Did you find your spark yet?"

This is the moment I could tell you what I can't believe you can't see.

I shove my paws into the hoodie that used to be yours, and tell you I'm fine, great really.

Stand up. I tell myself.

I try for words that are lost in a blizzard only I can feel. You look past me. Behind me is the café door, and behind that, a short street, front steps with chipped cement, and up some stairs, a place we came home to, back when there was room in our habitats for so many different forms of hope, both of us smiling, covered in salt.

What if we could go back there? Wasn't there a time when gray wolves came back to a forest? When dolphins swam in city rivers?

"Remember our first date?" you ask, abruptly.

Every word. We sat here and rebuilt the world, with gardens on rooftops. We would filter the air with our own lungs. We would raise coral where there used to be pools. We would comb oil out of feathers with our own fingers, and there would be time for love.

Maybe you remember it too, because you smile, and say, "We've been stubborn." The walls around us shift: café, snow, local artist's watercolors, ice field.

You'd think an ecosystem would be easy to fix, right? You just take the steps in reverse. Reabsorb the poisons: the byproducts of our fear, the toxic things we said; maybe a carbon offset for all my nights at the lab, for all the times we forgot to watch the sunsets we still had.

"What are you thinking?" you ask.

Your hand, so soft, is halfway across the table.

I am still looking for my strength in you, even as I can feel new muscles and sinews wanting to lift my skin like a sail across a dead ocean. Outside, a small man grips a lamppost with fingers and toes and turns his head almost the whole way around to blink at me.

I want to take your hand in mine.

But across the street, the bartender who gave us our drinks is standing on a balcony. The sun lights up her back like wings. Across the table, you lean forward. My claws catch on the inside of my sweater pocket.

"Are you going to say something?"

Ice cracking under my feet. Promise of cold below.

Your lips touch mine briefly. No words.
And when you get up to go, I find my all-fours.

*

Sealboy texts and asks if I want to come over. This time, I do. His jeans hug his little round belly, which spills over his belt, so soft and warm. I search his neck blubber for a vein, like tracing for water beneath the ice, and when I find it, I grow teeth.

*

I ride the train home under a full moon. At every station, when the doors open, I hear sounds I've never heard before — not cars, not horns, not phones, but howls, roars, guttural, creaking, inviting.

Not yet, I tell myself. I read our text history. I begin a message. I am looking for a word. The word is forgiveness. Or belonging. Or maybe something like kin, but not any of those.

Every letter takes focus. Ellipses, DNA strands, salty after-taste of sealboy, the smell of ocean around me.

One day, if all goes well, we, the ghosting, will enter a tall, ceilinged building with so many empty rooms, and we will spread out, and need only open our mouths and out of us will spring so much life: bison and beetles, quagga and sea anemones.

If all goes well.

Or maybe not.

Meanwhile, I wonder if there is still time for the chill to set in, for snow to cover our city. There might even still be time, I think, to fix things, or to learn to breathe life back into an ocean. Or at least to tell someone younger than me what a fish looks like. It looks like this, in case anyone wants to know:

Shiny blue thrift-store yarn, my grandmother's hands, a knitting needle through the gills, a knot tightening, and a warm jasmine-scented voice telling us something that if we could just remember it, might keep us real for the rest of our lives.

II. ~~Tales of The Sea~~
Tales of the Post Ocean

Letter from Maxxy at Now Collective to Cass at B. Collective

Cassiopeia My Love …

Jay was going to leave this book behind at The Paradise. I thought you'd like a distraction so you don't text Sam (Don't!).

How did B. Collective get those tickets? I heard B. hacked the Exodus. Jay says you just bought them. Maybe one day you'll tell me all of B. Collective's secrets.

Speaking of Jay … so much to tell you. You miss out when you're *always* in rehearsal. Lucky you have me on the scene. Here's what happened last night. Let me tell you like it's a story …

We're at The Paradise. Jay has one worn leather boot on the brass footrest, going on about the ship. I'm watching the dancers behind Jay trying to imagine half of us gone. Jay's quoting Butler back at me like I'm not the one who made them read Butler in the first place. "Maxxy, our destiny is to take root among the stars." They're drinking a cocktail from B. Collective, so it comes out "Starzzz."

Then the bartender stops cleaning the glass and looks at the door. Jay freezes like they're in an electrical storm no one else can feel.

Standing in the doorway is Seb. Seb with their long hair, the beard coming in, the light brown skin and eyelashes you can sweep the floor with, Seb looking like a thick femme Jesus!

Seb's not young. I see some gray hairs. Jay's not twenty either: gray is creeping into their perfect fade, and for all they love joking that they'll never age, there are in fact lines under their perfect cheekbones. Seb is walking across The Paradise in slow motion. The crowd is parting. Seb and Jay face one another. Seb smiles. Jay shakes their head trying not to smile. Seb steps forward. Jay doesn't step back. They have a year's worth of conversation in that one second. Then the power goes out. Again.

And when the lights go back on, they're kissing, like nitrogen + glycerin = BOOM.

No one saw that coming! Then again no one expected Exodus 3 tickets either.

Have you decided? Now Collective is #teamship. We're arguing. Exodus 1 exploded. Yes, Exodus 2 landed, but has anyone written back to say "it's great here?" No.

Then again, Earth is no picnic. Dion's missing. Mosh who used to bartend? Gone. RG says he saw a cat drag a body down an alley. RG exaggerates … But on the way home, I saw a paw print big as a manhole cover (manhole! So gender!) and the vine forest is growing.

How do you find home in a place you've never seen? Like when a friend tries to set you up with another friend and says, "You'd like one another. You should fall in love!"

We look at the fuzzy pictures. We read the stats: O2, Co2, N2, H20. We think about other times we had to leave something behind — a hometown, a lover, a whole kingdom beneath the waves. Anything can be a habitat, even just one person. Will you go if I go?

Maxxy

PS: I don't blame Seb and Jay … between the ship, the giant fucking cats and the creepy vines, we're all looking for second chances. Maybe you should text Sam.

~~The Little Mermaid~~ Playlist 4 Merx In Times Of Sea Levels Rising

Track 1: Elysia Crampton, "Crest"

Max found her own way to the ocean in her dreams. She did not follow the others, bent double, crawling through the endless dark pipes marked "To Beach." Instead, she navigated the high concrete walls of the cliffside city until she came to a hole in the ground, a frayed rope spiraling into the sunlight and ocean below. She climbed down carefully as the rope swung, feeling the burn of the rope on her palms. She stopped halfway and there she stayed clinging, wanting the ocean, afraid to let go.

I had the craziest dream, she said to the wrinkles in the empty bed. And then she made dry crying motions into her pillow.

"Where do you think these dreams are coming from?" the therapist asked.

The therapist was provided by the school where Max taught, and so she was reluctant to call him *her* therapist. His small cramped office was across the street from the school, window facing the flagpole. His chair creaked as he crossed one plaid pant leg over another.

Max's eyes fixed on the red and black plaid worn unironically.

"I don't know," she said.

As if they both didn't know.

As if the whole town of Inland didn't know. And the whole Internet.

Didn't know that ten days ago, Max had taken her Senior students an hour to the coast on a field trip. That while Max was busy leading a sandcastle contest, three of her students had walked out into the ocean, laughing, taking video, arm in arm. That their chain had been broken by a sudden tug of current, a rogue wave. That two students had been swept far away. That one boy, a *Jeremy* boy, had not returned.

It was all over the news:

… Coast Guard having suspended search …

… Missing Inland High Student …

"   "

the space in these articles where you could feel the reporter wanting to write *honors* student, which he wasn't, or *promising,* which he was, but not by their standards.

"   "

The absence of what should have mattered: that he had lived his seventeen years an hour from the coast and had never seen the ocean until that day; that he never seemed to have the right combination of books and crumpled handouts; that he dated this girl, Wren, who sat in the front row and had gemstones on her nails that glittered like scales; that Wren was pulled out of the water by the coast guard and wrapped in an orange blanket and lived.

The articles didn't say that Jeremy had actually read *Catcher in the Rye*, which most students hated almost as much as Max did, and had made a joke about it to her after class. Now he was out to sea and she could never tell him she appreciated that, would never put down her pen fifteen years in the future, astounded by the confident man in her classroom doorway, strong hand extended, *remember me?*

Then again, she wouldn't be here either. Not if she could help it. If she could have anything she wanted, she would be in her new life, up north in that coastal city. She'd be gathering artists, hosting literary readings, nowhere near a school. A bookstore, maybe: dusty Sunday afternoon light, chairs gathered, maybe a poetry reading, her friend Cass there smiling, and perhaps Max herself would get up, pull a poem out of her pocket, and —

The plaid pants. The present moment, with its terrible weight.

"Maybe I'm afraid of the water," Max fished, for the benefit of the notepad, for the benefit of the last week of school she had to endure, before the new life waiting for her, her sisters brothers siblings calling to her, her new life too long deferred.

"Maybe the divorce?" Her voice dissolved like a paper boat.

"The divorce was last October." He tapped his notes and crossed his plaid again. "Come on, man," he said to her, "You're not still driving to the ocean?"

Track 2: Bobby Darrin, "Somewhere Beyond The Sea"

Max was not dreaming when she left the therapist's office and drove to the ocean. She sat on the concrete wall above the sand looking into the salt mist over the blue, hoping for a wave with a face in it, a face, or better yet, a living Jeremy she could bring back to school and say *Look! I fixed it! Now can I go?*

[Skip]

Which is when she saw it, between two waves on a large rock. Like a magic trick:

Now the rock was empty.

[Skip]

Now there was a person there.

Jeremy? No.

Tbh, as Jeremy might say, it wasn't really a person at all.

Now the [skip] was gripping the rock, looking back at her, long hairs tangling —

like seaweed?

Cliché, Max thought.

Some trick of the light on the water made the [skip's] eyes look pupil-less, like black tide pools. The person in the water looked back and smiled, as if to say,

> *Hey, come here*
> *I have something for you*

Which was, tbh, the oldest trick in the book.

Max looked down at the beach to avoid needles and torn cans. She lowered herself from the wall, feeling the warm sand give under her feet. She looked back up. Just the bare rock, not even a barnacle. There were no boys. There was no figure.

She stood a while watching the horizon and finally turned back to her car.

¡Splash!

She heard that! Loud as an empty classroom chair. She turned back to the water.

Waves. Waves. Waves.

Nothing else.

"Grief," she lectured herself in the car, underlining the word three times in the whiteboard of her mind, and slapping it for good measure, the kind of thing that used to make her an *inspiring* teacher, a *teacher of the year,* "a heightened emotional state. A version of ecstasy. Or insanity."

She merged into a school of blue and gray cars, like her own. She

We

Went home.

Flew down to tell our brotherssisterssiblings

We found

the source

of our last tear

Track 3: The Little Mermaid OST, "Part of Your World"

To avoid her ex wife, who taught Science at Inland High, and to avoid the news vans still parked outside ("Mere days since the tragedy …") Max ate at her desk, blowing crumbs off term papers, distracted by a sound that must have been just the highway nearby — not the sound of ocean waves. You can't hear the ocean from Inland High.

Max closed and then opened the window. Still waves.

Brotherssiblingssisters! I saw!
Saw nothing
   Saw everything! I saw
What did you see?
   I saw One! Alone!
     What is the world up above?
Wait and see
   We're ready!
     We need one last
        One tear to rise
     The world up above is different
How?
     Up there, there is no we, only Ones
What?
     No we?
Down here, together-together
We lose pieces of the song
Torn by a propeller — pulled up to the sky — down through gray
cloud — puddle — river, lost
        Yes, but we come back
  Together

    We re-member

Max had plans. If she could just get out of Inland. She had Cass. Cass had an actor friend whose couch Max could sleep on. Cass was — what a thrill to say — *a woman like her.* Cass had come through town last fall, the lighting designer on a musical Max had taken her students to see. Cass had come out of the light booth to join the talkback: tall, long blue hair, gold hoop earrings, quoting Iris Murdoch (*time, like the sea*) and Max slammed with this feeling of recognition and joy almost greater than love. Their conversation had unfurled over email, then texts, and even postcards: Murdoch, then Murcof then Murakami (Takashi, of course) until finally, a thousand texts later, Cass had texted, "Just get out of there." "I'll try," Max had said.

Max might even have been ready to come out here, even in this town, where the name of her mother's bridal shop was still legible though the shop had been boarded up long ago. But not now. Not with news vans parked outside, spilling out reporters, just waiting for another thing to put in the "…"s. She could only imagine what they would say:

Extra! Extra! Drowned Boy's Teacher Transgender.

The teacher "who organized the field trip to the ocean." The "Teacher of the Year," wouldn't she like to comment? And so here we were. A week from graduation (theirs) a new life (hers). She only had to make it through. She only had to keep it all down, both the sadness and this new sense of possibility rising inside her. And still those waves like the din of student conversation in the hall but more distracting, almost like words.

We remember what we eat

 One Song:
 One time a sailor fell off his ship. "Can you swim?" we said
 No
 So we ate him. Drank his tears
Now he is not
  A Lone

Max opened a new browser on her phone and researched tidal surge.

Tidal Surge: A sudden ocean rise caused by climate change.

There was a social media video with a million views, "Inland High School Tragedy," that she knew she shouldn't click on.

She wanted to believe they could have avoided it, if they really tried. She wanted to believe it was their fault, Wren and Remy and Lauren's, for turning their backs to the ocean.

One song:

> *One time a sailor looked up and saw*
that the night sky was an
> *ocean lit up with fish*
> *A boat came sailing*
uMop əpısdn

> *On the ocean sky, and in the upside down boat*
> *was a ɹolıɐs who would not look at him*
> *We ate them both. Two tears*
> *Need one more*

Without a knock, the door to Max's classroom opened and here was the principal. Before the wave, Guy Artal could have been the principal from a sitcom: wore beige pants almost up to his armpits, laughed at jokes, calm, friendly, sun-in-his-face. Since, he had a school to save by any means. Max watched Principal Artal's posture: legs wide, arms down. She tried to mirror him while he talked at her punctuating every sentence with dude, man, bro, boss.

"It's not like we're taking away your award, man. You're still Teacher of the Year. But under the circumstances ..."

The circumstances being that the field trip had been her idea. The circumstances being that Jeremy had been her student. The circumstances being that she needed to get out of here before someone decided the wave was her fault.

> *One song ...*

"Did you hear that?" he asked.

"Hear what?" said Max.

And to get rid of him, Max had agreed to Say A Few Words at prom. Because it would look good. Because the press would be there. Because of the good name of Inland High. Because of the voice in her head that said, *you have no choice,* and *it's the least you could do,* and also *what if ...?*

Slam. The door behind the principal.

What if she could go to the ocean and find Jeremy?

If she could find him by prom, she would come out on stage, not as *Teacher of the Year* but as Max herself, fishtail dress accentuating her long legs, a green sequin bustier, and she would raise Jeremy's hand and release him to the disco lights and summer songs before walking proudly out of Inland High School into a sky filled with stars.

> *We found*
>> *The source*
>>> *Of our last tear!*

Max drew a wave on the corner of a paper and left her pen uncapped.

>> *Across the world, sea water expands as it warms.*
>>> *A bank of a glacier falls, wetlands well up*
>>>> *Just one more tear and the sea will rise.*

We have until next full moon to get the tear.

And/or/then/what?

> *Sea Foam!*
>> *Not funny.*
>>> *One song …*

Track 4. Ah-Mer-Ah-Su, "Stale Water"

Back at the beach, Max sipped from her coffee cup with that sea creature logo. As for her class, she'd texted something about a headache and turned off her phone. They'd find a substitute, if only an undercover reporter. He or she or they would get a behind-the-scenes exclusive in an actual classroom, twenty five faces staring at you or not looking at you, but still expecting answers, and nothing but a state-approved curriculum to offer.

Around her, surfers shivered out of their wetsuits or ran out with their boards, right past the sign that now said *Rip Tide, Danger*. The way we all do, she thought.

Look!

One alone!

We are not curious.

Sometimes we are curious.

We are not lonely.

Only interested.

Fascinated.

Sometimes angry.

Curious?

Fish?

Sometimes!

One fish eaten from its school, not lost, half found later.

One turtle found her way to spawning ground.

One whale swims north, one calf, bleeding propeller wound.

An eel pours out of a plastic bottle.

Curious!

It's back.

What's back?

The One alone is back.

A shiny gray-blue elbow emerged from the water, pointing up like a shark fin, playful.

"I can see you!" Max shouted. A surfer turned to look at her. The elbow disappeared. A pelican swooped. Max sat down, hard, on the sand.

"I'm not leaving until you come back," she said.

In the shallow waters to her right, near a craggle of mossy rocks and tide pools, a tangled seaweed head slid out of the water. First came the eyes, then the neck. The tide pool should have been too shallow for a body. Max did not hesitate. She stepped her way over the sand, a thousand potential knives or needles be damned, because finally here was something, someone, in the ocean looking back.

The face in the water was not quite human. The nose was perhaps a little long, the cheekbones a little flimsy, the cheeks a little sallow, the eyes still very dark.

Which is to say it was —

"Ohio," Jeremy would have said. "Weird," she corrected.

She stepped closer to the creature that should not be in the water, and that was probably a hallucination. Leaning over to talk to a hallucination, that's awkward.

Almost as awkward as driving up to your town's only queer bar one night, having always known it was there, but never thinking it was there for *you.* Awkward as seeing kids from Inland High in the parking lot, and then speeding away, and coming back. Awkward as imagining the clamor that would go up the minute she crossed the threshold, all the bright lights going on and everyone screaming *you don't belong here!* like a surprise party. But they hadn't.

The hallucination grabbed Max's forearm and pulled. Max had just enough time to see long scaly fingers around her arm. To dig her heels in. To see the sharp rocks piercing the shallow water. To think, "No, please no, I was just looking for the boy."

What boy?

The fingers slid off, leaving her arm salty and cold.

The one who belonged to the empty chair in her classroom. Who was always bobbing up out of his sweatshirt. *Can I turn in my homework tomorrow? It wasn't me who was talking. I'm not getting why this is important.*

Now, no matter how many times she rearranged the classroom, there was a gap between desks. A maelstrom of attention she could not look at or away from. Like the tide pool that now appeared empty, but rippled slightly. Max's boots slid over the rocks. She knelt to grip with her hands. When she looked down, the ocean looked back at her.

"Are you a hallucination?" Max asked.

Blue lips surfaced, smiled, puckered. Splash. A spurt of water caught the side of Max's lip. She tongued it. Salt.

Max wasn't out here looking for mermaids or mermen or anything. That would be ridiculous. She was looking for Jeremy. She was standing vigil by the ocean for when he swam back.

Two pupil-less eyes just under the surface stared at her, unblinking. A green purple blue tail swished, raising little currents.

~ ~ ~ ~ ~ ~ ~ ~

But if she was looking for mer-, that would be perfectly reasonable too. It was basic geometry.

<u>STATEMENT</u>	<u>REASONING</u>
1. Given the possibility of a mer person	1. Given
2. Therefore, the possibility of a raft just in time	2. If merx, then why not teenage boys?
3. Therefore, a chance encounter with a coast guard, also possible	3. If sea monsters with fishtail legs, why not teenage boys in hoodies, safe at home?
4. Therefore, a boy coming out of the water, unscathed, a week	4. QED

after the search party
ended, laughing,

5. "You thought I was   5. For the millionth time,
    dead, Mr. D!"   Max almost answered:

"Just call me Max."
Instead she said "If you're not a hallucination, then …"
  We are the ocean.
   A fish
     A predator
       A highly evolved symbiotic collective —
         Hungry
           Symbiotic collective in the shape of a female one.
             female One most of the time, because sailors
               A male One lots of the time,
               More often than you think
             because sailors
  Or maybe, just
           A fish
             Or two.
               Or sea foam
                 Which is boring
                   But useful!
                   a mixture of decomposed organic materials,
zooplankton, phytoplankton, algae,
         bacteria, fungi, protozoans, vascular plant detritus and mess
           Definitely mess
"If you're the ocean," Max said, "then give me back the boy."
                   Help yourself!
"What?" said Max.

Two waves crossed and a dark hole opened between them, spinning all the way down into the dizzying dark. Down there, unfathomable depths. Down there, creatures whose eyes had evolved into jaws, cold caves, spiraling light. Max stepped back. No.

The Merx laughed and then was gone. Nothing but tide pools and coral polyps, senseless mouths opening and closing obscenely with the tide, and seafoam, which is maybe all you get to be at the end. So why bother?

Max drove back to Inland. To avoid the school, the students trudging out with their backpacks, she drove through the residential neighborhood and found herself in front of Jeremy's house.

One tear, help the oceans rise

Jeremy's family lived in a brick and particleboard house painted yellow, smaller than it looked in the papers. There was a basketball net over the garage, hoop lilting to the left. The windows were dark, the door weathered from the wind that persisted in bringing in salty drops from the sea. She wanted to stop and say something, she didn't know what. But she already knew the door would be unlocked, would spring open the minute she stepped onto the gray peeling porch, that a ragged voice would ask, *Jeremy?* She knew this because the door to her unit in the courtyard condo was unlocked too, with a welcome mat and sand piling into the corners.

Cry.

Max did not cry. She could not cry. She hadn't cried all year.

She did not cry tonight as she came home, filed away final papers, made herself tea, and finally went to bed. Because of the ocean in her dreams.

The ocean in Max's dreams is ice-shifting, glacial banks thawing, a solitary fishing boat adrift. The ocean in her dreams is full of plastic, wedding dresses, *Catcher in the Rye*, and yet still so alive.

The ocean in her dreams is too big for the frame, and so it spills out, flooding her classroom, swallowing the school whole. The ocean in her dreams is filled with oil rigs, awe-inspiring and cataclysmic, like that butch at the Hook Bar's pool table, white tank top riding up her belly, one diamond stud, smiling, and Max wakes up. Network cables underskin like veins, thoughts scattering, dry eyes.

At least try?

Track 5: Tori Amos, "Silent All These Years"

Any decent reporter would know Max was far from Teacher of the Year.

Take the incident one day last fall. It was during what Max called her *working things out* period, less an epiphany than a number of small frustrations: The Revolt of the Clothes (when nothing in her closet seemed to fit), The Accidental Overshare ("Don't you wish you could just shapeshift?" Mister Ross, Phys. Ed. teacher, did not wish he could shapeshift), and a lot of driving to the ocean to feel the salt.

On this day, in a bright blue scarf that had felt necessary but also seemed to want her strangled, Max plodded through another section of the Iliad, a class she had taught, it felt, since antiquity: honor, valor, battle, Achilles and Patroclus, a love story?

When she unwound her scarf for the last time, she found Jeremy still in her classroom. He was agitated, throwing his notebook and backpack around, throwing his pens in, shoving his chair into the table hard. Wren, his girlfriend, looked at his face and walked off without him. Max wished she could leave too.

"I have a joke for you," Jeremy said, after a while. "I heard a really funny joke in soccer. It's really funny. Wanna hear a really funny joke?'

Before she could stop him Jeremy had launched into the joke, that old homophobic chestnut, *if you like fishsticks*. He said it twice, the delivery, and the punchline.

He stared at her, waiting.

That's inappropriate, she thought. Why are you telling me, she thought. Is it the scarf, she thought?

"We don't make those jokes here," she said weakly.

"You're right," he said, then he laughed. And his laughter let go the storm, made the joke another costume he was trying on, another version of masculinity he was shrugging off. And now he was lighter. She hadn't known you could just do that.

She should have said something else, but then came the next student who was waiting for Max, Wren's friend Lauren who would later take video of the wave, wanting to ask about the final paper, and *could she write about that pop star*, her red-painted nails gripped the phone that would later show everyone where Jeremy had gone, *because she loved that pop star, and thought she really had something to say about The Now*. And they figured something out for Lauren, who was actually a promising cultural analyst, and who just last week published a letter to the editor in the Inland Times on rogue waves and climate change and tearing down schools. Over the weekend, Max had read it, and almost cried,

!!!

but couldn't.

Now it was Monday, the last week of school. Wren was absent. Lauren was picking at the last few chips of red nail polish. No. She had to do something.

Max gave the class a reading assignment: Lauren's article.

While they read, Max ignored the *ding, ding,* of text messages echoing across the room. She researched riptides. To find a riptide, you have to look for places where the ocean is too smooth to be true. You have to watch for debris, like seashells, floating outward. You have to trust, because riptides take you far, but eventually bring everything back to shore like a trade. She ended class five minutes early.

On the beach, Max went looking for a riptide. She found one, like a runway down the middle of the ocean. She marched right up, ankle deep, feeling the pull, and slapped the surface of the water like she was calling a dolphin for a trick.

She didn't have to wait long. Close to her feet, too close for comfort, blue elbows reached from the water. Wrong. They hinged the wrong way, showing a vein ridge, an elastic joint. With a wet snapping sound, they popped inside out, and then there were hands — long fingers crawling the beach for hard sand — and then the Merx pulled themselves out of the water in a smooth slippery motion. Max jumped back, instinct.

The Merx took some hesitating jerky steps. Their legs were bloated and pale, veins bulging. A grayish waxy substance was beginning to marble the exposed skin where the fat was turning to soap, a fact Max wished she didn't know. One leg, the right, was paler than the other. The left leg bore a tattoo of a ship and tapered in a rugged tear above the knee. It was hastily stitched to a much thinner calf by rusty cables, the worst sewing job Max had ever seen.

Max blinked hard.

Now, the Merx was as ordinary as jeans and a flannel shirt. It/they looked solid, real, only perhaps a little wet.

Above, the skin remained that *no, but where are you from-from* shade of gray.

Florence! Max's parents would tell people they were from, even went as far as to call the bridal shop *Bambina's* even though Max's grandparents were from Oaxaca and they had a few second cousins there who still called. Max's mother had spoken bad-movie-Italian to the future-brides, *che bella, Massimo, get me the metro, I need to measure.*

In a fairy tale, the room full of wedding dresses would have been Max's awakening, but it wasn't. She hated the bridal shop. She hated constantly being reminded that in middle school, she had been the Bambina Boy. She hated how every future-bride who came to Bambina's had settled on one of the same three shapes, one of three shades of white/off white/pink.

"What if there's no other option?" Max asked, out loud. The Merx's lips, still slightly blue, smiled, creasing their large forehead. They still had a quality of being hard to see, the way that waves in the sunset are hard to see because they burn a million colors, but not hard to smell. The Merx stood at Max's height, reeking of brine, oysters, halibut, stagnant tears.

"What do you want for him?" Max asked.

The Merx smiled and walked past Max, looking back as if to say *COME!*, across the sand, toward shore.

"I didn't realize you could walk," Max said, looking around, absurdly, to make sure no one she knew was on the beach.

Water shapes to its container, said the Merx.

The moon is coming. Where is the tear?

One day, one day with the one who is so alone

Max followed the Merx's long strides, away from her car, to the boardwalk.

While she followed, she noticed things: the smell of fish and chips, of salt and grease, the ding of skeeball machines, the ntz ntz, the squeak of sneakers on that game where you die if you stop dancing, the pinkening sky. People looked at Max and the Merx a second too long and turned away, as if embarrassed.

So many Ones!

Max felt a cold, hard pressure as the Merx's hand wrapped around her forearm. If they saw the Merx, they would be wondering what this teacher-type was doing. If they did not see the Merx, then what did they see, exactly?

"What should I call you?" Max asked, looking at the gray hand around her arm. She forgot to remember that in some high school elective language class,

Ondine,

means

We Eat

and so Max was surprised when the Merx pulled her to the CrabbyShack restaurant with the red plastic chairs, pointing insistently at the picture of the *Mega Sea Bowl,* which came in a large basket lined with grease paper and cost Max $29.99.

The Whole Ocean is Our Menu

said the sign above the restaurant in big blue letters, grinning dolphins on either side.

"How can you eat those?" Max asked.

The Merx grinned and put a fried oyster in their mouth.

"If I had lost something in the ocean, would you know where it was?" Max asked.

No. Too wet, vast, salty, and
too complicated, not even translated
only half digested

Yes. no information is ever lost

One song: A dead seal pecked at by a crab,
a fish eats the crab,
a seal eats the fish

A fish eats, the crab eatsthefisheatsthefisheats
One song: once a gold ring thrown into the ocean
A fish swallowed the ring
The fish was taken for food
a girl found the ring
the prince married her
This was not our fault
"I should have taught him about riptides."

The Merx's hand on Max's was surprisingly warm, not fish-like, not like seaweed, but maybe like the way an octopus should feel. Max squeezed it back instinctively. It yielded, boneless, blood pumping.

What is "he?"
Come home
Cry

"Will you at least look for him?" Max felt her eyes begin to burn. Maybe the salt. The Merx launched forward across the table. More than one row of teeth.

We want.

Max stood abruptly. Her red chair tumbled. Behind the Merx, in the line to the restaurant's order window, Max recognized a familiar shape: beige pants worn too high, a shirt tucked in, a strong wide back, loosened tie. The principal. It was all too much. Max staggered away, not turning around, not stopping until she got into her car.

Come back.

One song: a starfish eats a sea urchin
It takes three days
Five days left before full Moon

By the time Max arrived back in Inland, she was convinced it had all been another hallucination. It was time to be normal. Do normal things. Make dinner. She had a craving for salt.

In the frozen section of the Inland supermarket, Max ran into Wren. She had a wetness in her eyes, since coming back without Jeremy.

"Hey," Wren said vaguely, looking at the frozen food.

Did he talk to you? Did you know him?

"Hi, Wren."

The machines whirred. I'm sorry, Max would have said, but couldn't, because Wren would say: it's too late to be sorry. It was your job to teach us, why didn't you teach us about the Ocean?

Fishsticks

Wren turned to Max. She sniffled. Her nose piercing was irritated. Her makeup was running, and still Max realized that Wren, with her glitter, her gems, her oversized pants, would never be a *Bambina Bride*. How had Wren survived here in Inland? How had any of them?

"You have something in your hair," Wren said. "Are you going for a long hair look now? Cool." Wren pointed up.

Max felt around her hair, pulled out a tiny fried tentacle. They stood way too long, Max and Wren, looking at it. What, really, was there to say?

What would it help Wren to know that the night Max had gone to the Hook Bar, Jeremy had been there, white tank top and blue jeans. He'd been there leaning against his car. He'd been there, lit by the parking lot lights, mouth on another boys' mouth. Max had retreated as fast as she could, but had time to see he was smiling, looking for once happy, for once like he hadn't forgotten his books.

Track 6. Shamir, "Ocean Eyes" (cover)

The next day, five days before prom, Max walked into her classroom determined to teach. She had a poem to read. ("*Break, break, break, On thy cold gray stones, oh sea*" …). She had discussion questions. She had a tall thermos of coffee.

She pushed the door open and stopped. There, in the middle of the room was Jeremy's chair, covered in nail polish, marker, glitter pen, lipstick, candles, mardi gras beads, playing cards, a joint rolled behind a conch shell. And a plastic ninja. And the name Jeremy.

Other chairs had been arranged around it. At the front of the class was Wren.

What now?

Teacher of the Year would have insisted, might have raised his voice, *siddown.*

But Max nodded.

We Re-member.

Max found herself an empty seat in the back row. There was a murmur, not unlike waves, as Max pulled a pen from her backpack and looked up at Wren, at the front of the class, nodding encouragement.

Wren passed a lock of hair behind a pierced ear. "I guess. Maybe. Let's just write a letter to someone we love."

Max started writing, Dear Cass, what if I can't leave?

Track 7: Sophie, "Is it Cold in The Water"

Max spent the last day of school, a Wednesday, with the Merx. She told herself they were looking for Jeremy. But there was something about being with the Merx, watching them roll in the waves and soft warm sand like seashells, that made Max feel if not weightless, then *sufficient.* When the Merx laughed, tiny blue hermit crabs fell from their mouth and burrowed into the sand. It took getting used to, but it was so much better than what came out of everyone else's mouth.

They walked together over tide pools, warm wet recesses full of sea urchins and life. The salty wind caught Max's lips. She noticed, when she wasn't looking at the horizon, where the Merx's flannel shirt slipped a little. The Merx was constructing themself in real time. Their skin was more human looking now, only a few tattoos in bits and pieces, here and there, the rest was smooth and warm. There were only a few patches, mainly around the collarbone, that didn't soften. Plastic.

They stopped in a place Max had never seen, a little cliff shielded from the city and from the ocean, where the wind had brought a patch of warm sand. Max felt the Merx's hand in the small of her back, a tide rushing in. And suddenly the air changed directions and Max lost the ability to speak.

"Wait," Max said.

The Merx came closer. Blue lips.

Kiss the girl.

Max felt the pull of something she could not name.

Then a wave came and took Max's breath away.

Underwater, everything was different, but especially the light, which came at her from everywhere.

One song: A parrot-
fish chokes on boy-
jetski-bleached coral

One song: a little plas-
tic ninja One boy won
at the carnival drops
from a school
classroom.

It falls through the
rain drain, bobbing
through the pipes, out
into the ocean, eaten
by a fish, eaten by a
bird. It takes a little
ninja stance in the
bird's windpipe, right
between its wings. The
bird dies.

One song: a shark
thrown back into the
water without a fin
does not swim

((Max))

One song: a white
dead coral reef

One song: a turtle
swims into plastic nets

"*Cry, and make the wave come,*" the Merx said, before the black
rubber tube swallowed Max's vision, and the light was gone.

Max opened her eyes, back on land. Alone.

One song: you have three nights left

Track 8: Christine and the Queens, "Tilted"

Three days before prom and Max had no idea what she could possibly say to the assembled school. *A few words*, sure. But which words? Max paced to the window and back, no sound of waves. She finally turned on her phone and found the video, and this time she clicked on it.

It was only 30 seconds:

Lauren's head looked gigantic, full in the frame, narrating: *We're getting out of here.* Wren and Remy were in the water dancing, jumping to the left, jumping to the right, and then both of them together, arms linked. Max saw it even before Lauren did: a giant wave. A wave the size of a house, the tip dripping and rippling like so many icicles, filling the frame, screams. Max put her phone in her desk drawer and slammed it shut.

Whose fault? Hers. Max had failed to teach her students about the ocean.

"Mr. D., tell us about the ocean," Jeremy could have asked.

"That's not in the lesson plan."

What if instead she had stood up and said, "Put down your books. Today, we study the ocean. It is endless and dangerous. It will break your heart. It will rub your edges smooth. Some of you will not survive. None of us are safe, but let us all sail"?

Instead, she had shuffled and shuffled the same old names: Julius Caesar, Lear, Gatsby, so many dead white lonely men.

"You're getting out of here soon," she could have said. "There's a whole world out there." She could have said. "Leave now," she said to Jeremy in the past.

The oceans are emptying, wide blue rooms filled with plastic instead of fish.

An oily bird lands on the waters.

Here, have a plastic ninja.

Track 9: Anonhi, "Why Did You Separate Me From The Earth?"

A fishing boat found Jeremy's hoodie in open waters. The Principal texted her a picture, and then told her not to tell anyone. Max sped to the ocean, stood there with her car keys still in hand.

"You ate him. Didn't you. Didn't you?" Max shouted.

Found!

"It's not the same," Max screamed. "How can't you understand that?"

A cargo of a hundred thousand yellow ducks runs adrift and scatters in the sea.

Not a single one is ever lost
No yellow rubber duck is
ever lost

"I never want to see you again," said Max.

"When you're ready," the Merx whispered, "I'll bring the wave." Max thought, *that's the first thing you've said out loud.* And then: how were they speaking before?

"Wait," Max said.

But the Merx was already floating away, waving the water with legs melting into a tail.

Think about it!

Max waited there until dark, the lights of the city behind her making the water look inky, solid. She called out and was answered by waves.

Why couldn't she could go down there, swimming with her strong legs, her growing hair flowing in the salt water? Max closed her eyes and imagined hands on either side of her, *come on, I dare you.* The seagulls were silent, the ocean was empty and smooth. Max got three steps in, feeling the way her skin parted the water but was never part of it.

She went home. She shut the windows. She added song after song from Cass's texts to a playlist that wasn't finished yet, but that one day would be so sad it would raise the sea and turn back time.

Track 10: Enya, "Orinoco Flow (Sail Away)"

Max wore a suit to the prom. It fit her legs wrong, constricting her motion, rubbing against her thighs. She was conscious of the plastic water bottles on the snack table. She counted plastic bindings on cans. She watched Wren dance in a ballgown she had torn up and sewn back together with fishing net. Wren had covered the puffiness of her eyes with glittering eyeshadow (like tide pools). Max watched Lauren, nails restored, pulling a notepad out from her tuxedo pants, writing something down. Maybe a song lyric. Max thought, *they'll be ok. No matter what.* They had so much to float them.

But now, finally, on a screen they had set up for this purpose, a montage about the school year. A giant portrait of her she hated, *Teacher of the Year*, and a little remembrance of Jeremy. The principal announced her, brought the microphone down from the stage to where she was, her back to the exit. Teenagers turned towards her, and teachers. Max stood still. Behind her, behind the pink and blue balloons were the double doors of the gym with their crash bar handles. Outside, the moon would be full, the ocean at highest tide. She pictured it now, so full of furious life: algae and shampoo bottles, beer cans and manta rays, gallon jugs of orange juice, beluga whales, bodies with their mouths wide open, cruise ships with polished oak balustrades. Maybe even a plaid fishtail splashing into the water.

Max took the microphone. The metal was cold. She flicked on the button. Well, if all else fails, she thought, there's always seafoam. Seafoam is information. Seafoam is interesting: plankton, pollutants, algae, decomposing matter, salts. Memory. Seafoam is a start.

"There is only one thing I want to say …" Max began. The doors did not swing open. Why did she think they would? She had nothing to say.

On the edge of Max's eyelash, in the silence, a single tear dangled. Somewhere not too far, an ice shelf shimmered and rifted. The room dissolved into drops: each individual breath. Every last separate, salted second. She felt the weight that ached every single muscle and pressed her lungs like water. The walls seemed to ripple.

It wasn't so much, she told herself, just one tear. Just one or two inches of water rising. Not a flood. Just an unspooling of blue velvet, starting at the edge of the map and working inwards, over the highways and megastores, over hospitals and schools. A wave so big it would blot out the sun. Max gripped the mic.

Imagine crying an ocean wave, one made of everything living: boys, clubbed seals, still fish, and maybe at the front, blue lips, black pupil-less eyes, sewn-together ifs, the face of love, a wave she could ride all the way to her sisterssiblingsbrothers in the coastal city, holding a cold soft hand.

Max looked over the students and teachers. She could easily find it, the ocean. It might always have been there, so big she might have been breathing underwater all along.

"… hold on to one another," Max said.

A drop of salt falls.

And then turned off the mic.

it travels the air, drifts into a cloud, rains down, dark shapes move through.

Wren would feel it first, the rumble.

Water welcomes.

Wren would stare behind Max and grab Lauren's arm, digging with her shiny nails. Lauren would turn too, as the crash-barred doors shook in their hinges, as the plastic glass in her hands fell to the ground.

Water remembers.

Max wouldn't even need to turn around.

Water belongs.

Note from Cass at B. Collective to Jay at Now Collective

Jay.

This your fairy tale book? We're clearing stuff out, making room for survivors. The big wave that hit South of the city last week was much worse than we thought. 27 new people showed up yesterday. Many more didn't.

Ali was among them. He walked 36 hours to get home. He says the sky went dark and when he turned around there was a wall of water big as a house. 10 feet high. He says everything is just gone: buildings, trees, all underwater. People had to clamber up the old Highway 101.

It's starting to feel like the ocean is not dead, just evolving. Maxxy says one day we'll look out and see a giant tentacle made of cables, dead fish, and plastic. Trash Kraken.

As for the ship, I can't decide yet; it's tech week! I know how it sounds, but that's theater people for you. The world will be ending and we'll be in rehearsal.

But I know some people with Exodus 3 tickets. I asked Cakes at Expresso. She looked me dead in the face. "Going." No smile. Nothing else. That's Cakes for you.

Maxxy wants to stay now. At least I know I'm useful here.

Last night I rigged up an old lamp post with 4PV cells and an inverter, and now Heare Street has light at night. Keeps the cats away. From up there, I could almost see where I grew up, and it still feels like home, even though on one side, there are vines as far as I can see, at least 2 sq. miles covered in green. On the other side, the ocean is still there.

Sam swears they saw a boat. Maybe there's other places. Lagos, New York, New Delhi. A world out there.

Don't know if Sam's going. We're not talking. Maybe we'll talk after opening night.

Guess we still have time. 8 days. 192 hours to decide to go 192 million miles.

The furthest I've ever been is Inland, barely 100 miles away. When I put it in numbers, that's when it hits me.

Cass

Community Count:
T-Minus 8
#TeamShip: Jay, Cakes, Ali, 24 people who escaped the wave
#TeamEarth: Me (Cass), Maxxy, Seb
Missing: Dion, Mosh, a lot of people we know from Inland
and west of Inland. It's gone.
Remaining Tickets: 73 exactly, going fast.

III. ~~Tales of Bravery~~
Tales of the Post Fire

Dear Seb,

First, let's forget about the other night at The Paradise. I acted irresponsibly. You still kiss the same way, as if there will never be water in the world ever again — but I should not have kissed you.

Second, I don't think I should tell you what I've decided about the ship. I don't appreciate your implication that I leave things behind. Of the two of us, you are the one who forgot my birthday, who forgot to water the little brown garden you insisted on starting, who was always late to our dates and always with some fantastical story when we all know you just couldn't stop reading on time to get ready, who missed KC's memorial. You evaporate like ozone when things get hard.

Let's leave things on a good last note. I did love you, Seb. I remember when we started Nowhere. It was just a cardboard box you found behind The Paradise. You found a pen and wrote "FREE" on the side. KC saw it and put a few masks in. Cass took a mask and left a flashlight. Ali took the flashlight and left two joints and you panicked because you didn't know what to do when people kept arriving with offers and asks. We made a good team.

I liked making a place out of Nowhere with you. I will take that memory with me. Whether I stay or go, I mean.

I know you don't like to hear it, Seb, but there is no *Happy Ever After*. Everything changes, everything adapts. Even Capital-Letter-things like Love and Home and World. They were just verbs all along: things you have to do and make, and show up for.

Please take your book back. You know I do not like carrying non-essential things.

Take care,

Jay

PS: You should post about Dion on the wall at The Paradise.

Full Color Illustration

In an underwater cave, The Little Mermaid gazes at a sunken statue of the prince and dreams of a world beyond the sea.

Last Five Years According to the Bathroom at The Paradise, Drawn by Maxxy, T-Minus 7

The same way you can see in layers of rock and soil when there was an ice age or a drought, you can tell on the bathroom door where the world kept on ending and not ending in different ways.

TOUT POUVOIR
À LA BASE
REMATRIATE THE LAND – FUCK YOUR BINARY – STOP AI – TRANS
GIRLS RULE – BLOW YR PIPELINES – ACAB – GENTRIFIERS GO HOME
– NO BORDERS! – SAVE THE OCEANS – SAVE THE ORCAS – RIP ORCAS
Has anyone seen Mosh?
Anyone need another person in their collective?
I was an EMT.
Oys, if you see this, write back.
DON'T LEAVE PEOPLE BEHIND.
I'll wait here.
Giant cats are not friendly. Stay away from the giant cats.
BOYCOTT GALACTIC EXODUS 1!
RIP Exodus 1
Reach for the moon, you'll land among the stars.
GOOD LUCK, EXODUS 2!
IN PIECES
RIP TIGERS
Jay and Seb
made out here.
RIP Ocean.
EXODUS 2 IS LIES!
Beware the vines.
They have hyperpollen!
PLEASE READ:
We have 100 80 60 40 tickets to Exodus 3
Provided by B. Collective
SAY NO TO EXODUS 3
RIP EARTH LET'S GO!
If you wish to be considered for one of
these tickets, please talk to Cass at No
Exit Theater, or to Cakes at Expresso.
COLONIZER
You're welcome! — B. Gay Do Crime
Have you seen Dion?
Collective
Last seen at The Paradise on Thursday.
8pm Show At No Exit
Theater Tonight! Buy-
Contact Seb.
One-Get-One-Tickets!
Come see your last Earth-
play!

Dear Jay, as in Just Hold On While I Save
The World,

NOW you want to remember things?

KC was a friend to both of us and they're
still out there somewhere. So are Dion and
Mosh. You're so quick to give up hope, to throw
things away and be done with them. I know
they found new collectives beyond the vine
forest. I'm just too allergic to get through.

Just for the sake of argument, let me make a
wild guess: you're getting on the ship and telling
yourself it's human destiny, when really you just
have to have the next thing: disrupt, new app,
new clothes, new relationship every three
months (it's common knowledge). J as in Jump,
Jet, and why don't we Just find a new planet if
this one doesn't work out exactly as we wanted
it to.

I'd hate this about you, but it's why you
were always the first to go rappelling into sink-
holes and running into buildings after
earthquakes. Everyone knows how brave you
always are. Do they know you're afraid of the
dark?

No one said I was trying to follow you on a
seven-month space flight. It's hell bunking with
you. You snore, you sweat, you wake up at 2am
with all these demands (Sex! Snack! Story!
Seb!) you won't ever let anyone sleep until you
sleep. If we were both on the ship, they'd have
to throw us out the airlock.

I mean, theoretically.

But how can you stand to say goodbye to all this?

Don't answer that. I've seen you walk away from Paradise once, twice, even just last week, and not just the bar.

Nevermind,

Saint Sebastian the Persecuted

PS: Came to The Paradise to post on the wall. Didn't expect to see you there. And in such gorgeous company too. I like new-me #36. So guileless. Please give me the book back after you read this.

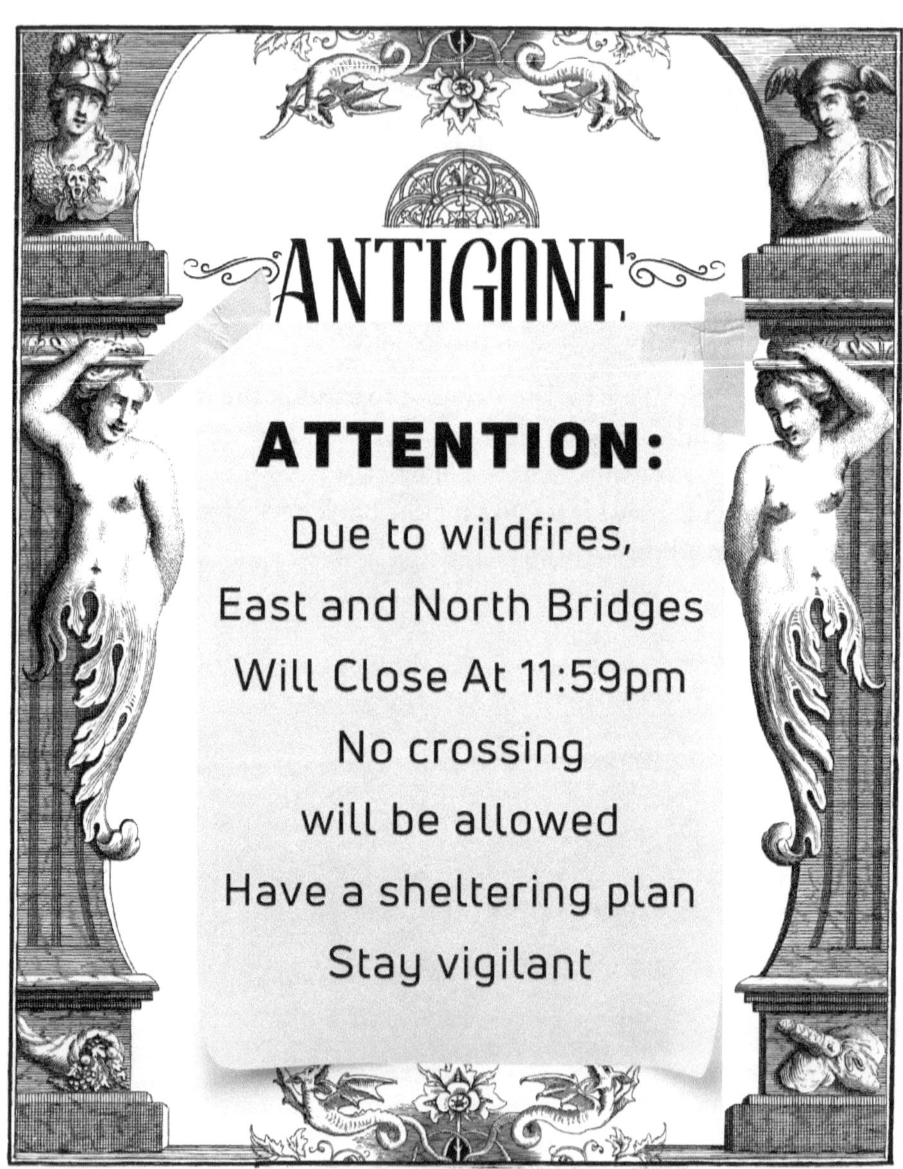

Sign posted on lamp posts on Heare Street

Dear Seb,

You are sometimes such a petty bitch/ bastard.

First of all, you are misusing *guileless*. The word you are looking for is undramatic. Yes, Maxxy is uncomplicated. No, she is not a new-you because Maxxy and I are not dating. Not that it's any of your business.

Second, I did not walk away from you last week. You ambushed me with this book and with your — body.

Third, you do not need to tell me you're staying on Earth. We've met. S is for Stubborn. Like that dead spider in your window you tried to feed for months. Like that story you made us read about the woman who dies just to bury her brother. Stories indoctrinate us into abstraction: honor, valor, kindness, loyalty, country, Earth, home.

I'm at The Paradise waiting for the show at No Exit. Out the window is one of those self-driving ice cream trucks. The truck is on its side. The windows are blown out. Vines are already beginning to wrap around the wheels. I haven't been inside to check for bodies or supplies. Maybe I don't always want to be brave or heroic. Sometimes I just want — I don't even know.

Maybe I'll find it out there. I wish you would come too.

Because of the vines, I mean. You're aller-
gic. It's common knowledge. Please go tell
Cakes you want a ticket and stop writing to me.
I'm giving this book to Ali to take back to B.
Collective. Go get it from him. Keep your
heroic stories.

Take care,

Jay

~~The Brave Sister~~
Antigone, But With Spiders

I. Tech Week and the World is On Fire Now

Never ever ever not ever again. That's what you tell yourself every single goddamn time. When this is all over, you say every time, you're going to get an adult job, in an adult office, where people act like adults. Yet here we are, eating stale pretzels around an empty stage dust mote circus, because Antigone is late to *Antigone*. It's just rehearsal, but technically, rehearsals are how you get to the play: you rehearse, then you take pictures, then people come see the thing you spent months rehearsing. Except at this rate, there won't be a show at the end of the week. In other news, the photographer is afraid to leave his house. Most people are these days. The voluntary evacuations have begun, neighborhood by neighborhood. You wonder if Antigone has evacuated. You wonder why you haven't.

You pretend to call Antigone on your phone, but you know she's not going to answer because also absent is Marc, set designer, who is supposed to be building Thebes in this theater, and you know they've been drifting closer these last weeks. *Timing!* and also

Placing? because, where are they? It's not like they can just go out and have a picnic, it's not like anyone in this city can host, not with the checkpoints. It's not like they can kiss, not through the masks. Marc is cute, in his little mustache, but Marc is not permanent-lung-damage cute. The mercy is that his post-modern minimalist Thebes is only half built, so they're probably not hooking up in the foam palace. Or the super metaphorical sandbox. Oh God.

Everyone is thinking, *can we leave? Can we go home to our snacks and filtered air?* Everyone is reaching into their backpacks and brushing lighters or joints. Everyone is nodding to fiddle their phones. Everyone is one step away from fiddling themselves, except The Great Director, who is recently back from some fancy primal-screaming-in-leotards retreat, and is about to make A Speech.

You look up to the sound and lights booth at the back of the theater and roll your eyes, reflexively, like you shouldn't anymore, but the booth is behind a dark glass. Not even a metaphor. And it's most likely empty. She — capital S — the sound & lights tech, has been timing Her — capital H — arrival around your departure. Space is healthy. Boundaries lead to friendship. Shoes keep you from throwing yourself onto the ground and screaming. In a locked room inside your ribcage, spiky cold infinities unspool and unspool next to a dusty projector, dark-covering a floor no one will ever see again.

~ Adaptation Ideas ~

Today, but without crying for thirty minutes before work.

Antigone, but King Creon sends Antigone a condolence card and observes the comfort-in-dump-out model of crisis response.

The Sound of Music, but without Nazis and without monogamy, just the Captain, the Baroness, and Maria raising their composite family and taking in lots of foster kids besides.

Aida, but with Tardigrades. After being buried alive, the Captain and Aida live happily underground, emerging two hundred years later. Maybe not even emerging at all. Who needs to go anywhere when you're in love?

Creon, the actor playing Creon, has five mini cookies in his mouth because he's stoned, has been consistently stoned for a month, and you can't blame him. Between Ismene and the Great Director, he is steadily being micro-aggressed to death. Leaning over him is Polyneices who is twenty, on summer break from Stanford where both his parents teach, and here for school credit. Being the least important member of the cast, Antigone's dead brother, Polyneices feels entirely justified taking up all the space, like now, cornering the Great Director to extrapolate on a paper he wrote about *Antigone* two semesters ago.

You can't figure out why Polyneices is here at all, being that his entire character is dead, and there are plenty of other things an intern could do, you think, than play a corpse that could easily be a bag, which would at least be silent, because now he's going on about *the chorus as groundswell we,* and *the brevity of our moment in the spotlight of life,* which brevity you sometimes wish you could accelerate for him, tbqh.

"I can read for Antigone, if you want to get started," you suggest again.

"Huh?" the Director says, because he's been raiding Creon's stash.

"Antigone is late," you remind him patiently. (Mood: Happy Stage Manager with a Heart of Gold). "I can't reach her."

"We could start rehearsing the scenes without Antigone first," says Ismene, Antigone's sister in the play, Little Miss Helpful on a Bulldozer. Ismene was here so early, you had to leave the coffee line to let her in. Ismene has been early since day one with her script pre-highlighted, her shoes matching her handbag, and all the air sucked out of the room and stored neatly in alphabetically labeled containers.

You resist the urge to point out that in *Antigone*, it's kind of important to have Antigone, being that the play is *Antigone*, but then the broken ceiling fan turns on suddenly, like it does, catching a light that swings and glimmers off the soundbooth glass, and for a second it looks like She might be in there.

The Sphinx, but its only riddle is, "how will we survive now that all is gone?"

"Do we have everyone else?" the director asks you instead of counting.

Everyone else is here, the full set. Polyneices, the Very Important Corpse, the brother Antigone sacrifices her life to bury, is very much here. He's on his phone trying to show Ismene some Recent Internet Thing. King Creon, who decrees that anyone burying Polyneices should be executed, is here, tapping his phone, probably desperate to see if anyone else is hiring. No one else is hiring. Also present is Haemon, Antigone's fiancé, who does not-much until Antigone dies, and then kills himself. In real life, he's mostly about going to the gym and motivational quotes. He's playing the phone game where you line shiny things up to make them disappear. Antigone's sister Ismene is here, all attention, when she's not making eyes at Haemon or Creon because she cannot pick up literally one cue, and has not noticed she is the only straight person in this room other than The Great Director. In this production, the chorus is played by a projection onto the back wall because: budget, and also, modern. Another adaptation.

"You'll read for Antigone then. Let's take a break. Places in five."

"Thank you, five," we respond, because we're all trying to sound like Professional Theater People. Even though the other theaters have boarded their windows and shut down, even the main theater with its faded and soot-covered posters for *Annie!* and all the jokes about *tomorrow* that just write themselves now, don't they?

2. Stage Left

There is a spider on the toilet seat of the gender neutral bathroom: eight black legs splayed on the ceramic, small body preparing to skitter, most likely onto your face. You decide it's not worth it. You step out of the stall and wait.

Creon walks in, sees you, walks out, walks in again, confused.

You avoid the mirror on the way out. The "I" that is no longer viable as an "I" lives in that mirror. Most people, they think you need an *I* to do things, like go to work or order coffee, but for a while now, you've been just fine with a *you. You* can be a stage manager. *You* can help Antigone with cues. *You* can take attendance and watch. The only thing *you* can't do is just magically become a happy person beloved by all. Some adaptations work and some (*Macbeth, but in space*) don't. But you can have a practical working relationship with this *you*, no better or worse than your relationship with the Great Director, Ismene, Creon, and for now, *you* is enough.

The Sphinx, but with affirmations instead of riddles. It says, "what you are is fabulous, and that's what you are." It says, "the thing that walks on any number of legs belongs."

Back on stage, we go through the whole drama again. Polyneices died in the civil war. Creon decrees Polyneices' body shall remain unburied. Antigone says she's going to bury him. Ismene says, *no please don't.* Antigone buries Polyneices slowly in our very expensive sandbox. Creon sentences Antigone to be executed. She hangs herself instead. A curtain reveals her body, your body in this case, and everyone screams.

Half-Built Thebes was supposed to be a palace (barely a frame) a few columns (nonexistent) and a giant pile of sand, the metaphor being that the land was begging for burial. A month ago, when the sand was delivered, you and Sound & Lights stayed up late rolling and burying one another, laughing under blue lights. It's good sand, so fine it runs right through your fingers in this used-to-be palace.

At lunch break, you and Ismene dig up Polyneices, who can't get out of the sand alone. Costumes come off, masks go on. You unlock the theater door. It's still daytime, but not light, more like dark gray.

Ismene's mask is designer, matching her shoes and handbag. Haemon is wearing a bandanna, which doesn't do much for him one way or another. He's been coughing lately. Polyneices' mask is silver, matching his silver glasses, making him look like he's going to some extraplanetary math club rave. Creon's is standard issue and small on his face, but he reaches into his pocket and hands an extra mask to a magenta-haired woman in a wheelchair, who blesses him with a raspy voice.

The sun, through the ash, turns the world Thebes-orange. The wind is picking up, which means the fires will spread, which means another thousand people will lose their homes and lives, but that's beyond the scrim of the city limits, where people are numbers and no amount of imagination will make them feel like people. There is a person lying on the ground, but you're too scared to see if that person is asleep. What would you do anyway? You don't know CPR. Your degree is in Dramaturgy, adaptation. The air is aluminum and your throat is a microwave and everything crackles. You put on the mask that is Her mask that you stole from Her house and finally you can breathe.

The phone buzzes. *A do over. A second chance. Two tickets to Paradise.*

It's Antigone.

Her off-stage name is Jessica. You pick up and say, *Jessica, are you ok?* and you make it sound like *what the actual fuck?* because you're a great stage manager.

But it's not Jessica/Antigone. It's Marc, builder of, slacker of, Thebes. He's at the hospital. He's with Jessica. She's on a ventilator. You let him talk the air out of a sad balloon. You can't remember a time when news of people on a breather was surprising, but there must have been, last year, or last month. You remember standing in line for masks. You remember when jokes about the apocalypse stopped. You remember saying things like, "hey, it's the end of the world, can I get you a drink?" and you remember that line sometimes working, dive bar lights catching you like an event horizon.

The Director is briefly #sadface about Jessica and then too-quickly decides you can be Antigone. You tell him fifteen iterations of "I'm the stage manager," but it's no use, because no one knows the part like you do, and it's Wednesday, and the play opens Saturday. You turn your back to the theater, preparing to deliver the no that will send everyone home for good, the one that rolls in your mouth like a grenade pin, and that's when She arrives to work the soundbooth.

The Sphinx, but smaller than you imagined; size of a pre-war building.

Her mask is green. Her hair, once blue, is now flame red, half short, half long.

Adaptation: The Break-Up Haircut.

She opens the theater door, looks back at you, nods once, turns away.

Hi!

you say, a brick trying to fly. The door bounces shut again.

Your life, but in Thebes. Thebes is nice. It has no laundry, only sand.

In Thebes, you can be illuminated by a sun that is your ex in the sound and light booth while people pay to see your heart break on stage.

A break up, but so well lit, you overcome your differences and fall back in love.

For the rest of rehearsal, you are Antigone, flickering back to the here/now to correct a line or remind Ismene to stand back a step. Polyneices, dead, can't stop coughing. Everyone comes in on the wrong cue. Rehearsal ends. The director tries a pep talk. The loud ceiling fan starts up, mercifully drowning out his words, so he shakes his round head like it's all a big mystery and says, *see you tomorrow.*

You take 3 buses home. On bus 2, a man leaps into the front windshield and slides off into the dusty air. The bus driver puts her head on the wheel. The other two passengers look at you, trying to roll eyes, trying to cry. You look away.

3. Tech rehearsal: The One Where We Turn the Lights On and Off

No one knows how to turn off the single bulb above stage right. Ghost light, they say, but even ghost lights have switches. This one flickers and flickers but never goes out. No one knows how to turn off the ceiling fan that whirs up at all the wrong moments. You're staring up at the fan pretending to fix it because today is Tech Rehearsal, and the Director is late.

The door opens, we all look up. It's not the director. It's Polyneices. We'd forgotten about him. Polyneices says, "good morning everyone" and then throws himself face down on stage. He wants to be here so much, even just to be dead, it's almost embarrassing, but Haemon grins and says, "Let's do some acting, shall we?" He leads Ismene and Creon to Thebes by the hands, skipping like Dorothy, and for a second they are happy. They call you, Antigone, up to join them.

We stand on stage while Lights, in the booth, whose name is Cass, whose name you can totally say out loud without crying no problem, says, "take it from the top of the scene."

Cassandra?

Cassiopeia.

We speed through the play like a bad explanation, like "It didn't mean anything," like "That's not what I said." Cass, Sound & Lights, interrupts to change the lighting. The tiny spark of joy dies.

A few months ago, we all believed in Tragedy as artform. It seemed a good idea to make Serious Theater, give our audiences a shake. Blue skies were still possible. Fires were just normal fires, and fire season was going to be a reasonable tragedy: a few hundred people losing their homes, a few hundred miles away.

The *No Exit* was our theater. Dusty, close, a cheap theater. The kind where you can bring your drinks in with you and your feet stick to the floor because everyone else did too. The kind where you can sit as close as you like and no usher is needed because there are only 15 rows. There was rain, water literally falling from the sky, and on the first day, you dragged a bucket on a towel to catch the drops from a leak in the ceiling, plink, plink, *show business!*

"What do you think of when you think of Antigone?" the Great Director had asked the newly formed cast and crew, nodding us along, excited to get to the part where he could talk about what he thought of Antigone. The theater's Artistic Director was next to him, smiling, both of their stylishly shaved heads catching the light. Sometime in the last few months, the Artistic Director moved himself and his family out of town. If the dust and smoke clears, if he ever comes back, he might be happy to know he still has a theater, that we're all still here, doing shows. Unless he moved to one of the safe areas that wasn't safe at all. Maybe it was his beach house on the news, flames crawling up the tall gates, smoke like a bat swarm, news anchor struggling to find words for fire that seemed to have evolved and could not be put out. "Superfire," "Megafire," "Magna Fire," or just "well, shit."

"Stubbornness," Creon had said. Creon is a dad and a Daddy. His dad side meant an endless repository of dad jokes and frantic calls to his daughter that mostly began, "No, you canNOT." His daughter evacuated east with her mom, and doesn't call anymore. His Daddy side means he was well known in the leather community, his face on a flyer at The Paradise, *International Mr. Leather.* His phone was busy once. Some days, he left early for PTA meetings. Other days, he left for the gayborhood with eye smile like someone just brought him the dessert menu. That day he leaned back in his chair in his #1 Dad sweatshirt, his leathers creaking beneath, and when he said "stubbornness," it sounded like "love."

"Sacrifice," Ismene said, drinking bottled water with charcoal in it. Ismene has, or rather had, a job in marketing and another in vitamins, and you were the only one unsurprised to find that she smokes, always at least one cigarette before going on stage. Ismene looked around to see if her word was perfect, and then asked Haemon to move his elbow so she could arrange her sushi.

"Strength," said Antigone/Jessica, coughing delicately into a red bandanna, at least that's how you remember it. Allergies, she must have said.

Polyneices had notes prepared. You almost didn't mind because Sound & Lights was in the room. You told yourself you would hold eye contact with her and you did, while Polyneices was talking, all the way from "fatal flaw" to "catharsis," until your chest melted into your stomach and you called break five minutes early.

"I'm getting coffee," you said, looking at her.

"I'm coming!" Polyneices said.

"You're the stage manager," Lights said later. "I'm Cass."

"Cassandra?"

"Cassiopeia. You?"

{Choose Your Own Adventure!}

Door #1: Use your old name. Let its steel wool wear down your features until you have no more need for a name;

Door #2: come up with a new name on the spot; What is the word you think of when you think of Antigone?

Sam, you choked out finally, stage manager with a vowel, giving her a handle by which she could pick you up and hold you and later drop you to pieces.

Now, at tech rehearsal, the stage lights are unforgiving. Or maybe you are just unforgivable. There must be a version in which everything is forgivable.

Oedipus, but with Mrs. Robinson, and when everyone finds out his great crime, they shrug and say, "that's terrible, but we can't blame you."

Romeo and Juliet, but with cell phones. Their elopement succeeds. Nobody dies. They move to a small apartment in Milan. They love and hate one another their whole lives, sheltered from the cold, touching all the old familiar walls.

As Sam, you were brave. You invited Lights out for a drink. "You know, because I didn't get to hear what you think of when you think of Antigone."

Any reasonable chorus would have facepalmed in unison.

You walked to The Paradise in a graying city. A man stumbled into your path and said, "hey ladies" and he said it deliberately because everything about you says, "don't call me lady." You hovered over your body dropping little missiles onto the street until the whole thing was covered in smoke. *Burn.*

Now the world is on fire and no one can breathe. Everyone feels guilty because everyone can point to a time when they wanted this, or something like this.

Creon says his line for Sound & Lights, in the same voice he once used to tell his daughter to stay home, be safe. His brow furrows. Responsibility stoops him.

Ismene's next. When she isn't moving, when she isn't rubbing something into her hands, or asking questions that aren't really questions, when her mouth is shut or speaking lines that aren't hers, she can give a sense of the deepest listening. You're sure she has a sister. They must braid one another's hair and laugh. They must call each other every single day.

Polyneices asks from the ground if Cass needs him to light check. She is kind when she says no. She was kind when she finally said no to you too.

You fell in love with Cass because when the Great Director asked her what she thinks of when she thinks of Antigone, she said "memory." You fell in love with Cass because when she came to your first date, after rehearsal three, she showed up disheveled on purpose, her blue hair lifted in places and falling in others, the top button of her jeans casually unbuttoned. "How did you get here," she asked, meaning Thebes, but also theater.

C.V.

1. The one where you played a tree, now extinct, in a kindergarten play about ecosystems.

2. The one where you were a princess forced to kiss a boy and everyone thought it was cute when the teacher pushed your heads together on stage, and even that couldn't diminish your love for the smell of backstage: wood shavings, sweat, old electrical wiring, glue.

3. The one in college where the girl you loved fell off a scaffolding hanging stars. With your back turned, you heard the scream-thump and could only think, "stage left. It's stage left."

4. The one that wasn't a play, but a memorial for this girl, where you helped people to their seats, and realized that this is what theater is: the thing you do when crying isn't enough.

5. The dozen or so plays you worked just waiting for a better ending or transcendence until —

6. The one where Cass took the booth and made even light feel tender.

"By accident," you said, lying and telling the truth at the same time. "And you?"

"Please the living, love the dead," she said, electrifying the line that Jessica/Antigone could never get right. You laughed because she had to be lying too. No one does this out of Love, right?

She asked, *what are your plans for fire season?*

Because fires were starting and there had been no rain and the chaparral was dry and everyone knew it was going to be bad, but no one thought it was going to be so bad you can't joke about it. We talked about fire season so reasonably, the same way we said things like, "If it doesn't work out, we can totally still be friends."

You shrugged and said, "staying." And you kissed.

Stage Directions: Now. Thebes. *Antigone stands alone, looks at Polyneices.*

Polyneices coughs, hot wind dry shrubs.

"Lights, could we pause for a break?"

"Oh sure, Stage."

"Thank you, *Cass.*"

"You're welcome, **Sam.**"

[Cymbal Crash].

⚜

There is another spider in the bathroom, this time on the sink. It's gone when you're done drinking.

Ismene walks in with a makeup bag.

"I'm sorry about you two," she says. "It'll get easier."

North of the city is on fire. South of the city is flooded. West is the Ocean. The roads eastward are clogged. Ismene puts death-mask-grade foundation on.

The rest of the day, you sit to run cues, the script open in your lap.

Stage Directions: Now, Location, Thebes. Enter Haemon. Exit Ismene. Enter Antigone. Lights. Lights.

NOW	ONCE
Location: Thebes *Enter Ismene and* *Antigone* *Exit Antigone* *Enter Chorus* *Enter Creon* *Enter Messenger. Exit* *Messenger.* *Enter Antigone. Antigone:* *Creon* *Enter Ismene* *Exit Antigone,* *Exit Ismene,* *Exit Guards* *Enter Haemon,* *Exit Haemon* *Enter Guard.* *Enter Chorus. Exit all.* *Thank you.* *Good work, everyone.* *Go home, get some rest.* *Exit all.*	*Location: Thebes. Sand.* *Enter Sam. Enter Cass.* *They kiss. Beat.* *Cass reaches for Sam in a way that* *feels wrong. Sam brushes her hand* *away.* *She moves her hand to Sam's back,* *between their shoulder blades. Beat.* *Sam holds Cass's wrist too tight.* *She twists her wrists strongly away,* *pulls back. Both breathe. Both* *apologize. Both wait and then* *continue.* *Sam and Cass memorize the shape* *of one another's scars. Here's where* *there used to be water and the* *water is gone, here's where there* *could be water again. They follow* *the scarred earth carefully back to a* *place where there could be water.* *Come home with me.* *Exit both.*

4. Opening Night Minus One, When Everything is Supposed to Come Together

They are closing the bridges and highways at midnight.

At home, you listen to the news and ask again for the mirror to name you, but no names come.

I is Leaf

I is Sam.

I is — **Coward.**

One morning last month, you woke up wheezing in the smoke. You texted your ex who lives in a place where the air map is still green. She sent you money for one bus ticket. Wouldn't anyone leave if they could?

A scene you see, over and over, as if through eight eyes: the bus ticket, the bag in your closet. Escape pod for one, and Cass, closet door open, taking it all in at once, "I thought this meant something to you."

Now, the night before opening, you text every actor to tell them the show could be canceled. You tell them to stay home. The bridges are closing at midnight and the show is tomorrow, but you could be on a bus out of the city. A small black spider crawls out from under your coffee mug. You catch it in your hands and hold it there.

One by one, the actors text back that they're coming. The ones who live across bridges will sleep at the theater. No one knows whether there will be an audience, but the show is on. They are all so much braver than you. You look down at your hands, and at least they look right, neither feminine nor masculine, but strong, covered in stage paint and splinters.

You open your hands to let the spider go, and begin to gather your things.

We are building Thebes ourselves. Haemon, it turns out, has a mind for shapes. He finds a block of foam that used to be a snowman and carves something vaguely Theban. Marc texts us from the hospital. Jes is awake. We videochat. We promise to come see her. We will rehearse in the hospital, in her room, on her bed. We will put on a show. A light comedy. *As You Like It,* but without the gender. She tries to keep us on the call, but we have to go. Now we are in this *we* without her.

Thebes is a burnt up landscape, but to us, it feels like a place. Polyneices makes a suggestion that actually works. Creon kisses him on the head, and turns to ask the director. This is when we realize the Great Director is gone. We carry on without him.

We find old vodka and toast what has come before:

The rehearsal where we couldn't stop laughing;

The one where everyone called Haemon "hey, man;"

The one where everyone was cranky, and Ismene literally stomped out the door;

The one where 100 pounds of sand arrived and you and Cass hung lights into the night.

The one where you waited in the hallway for her to come out, and when she did, she brushed past you without saying a word.

5. Opening Night: The One Where The Audience Claps

We spend the night in the theater, sleeping bags in the green room and on stage, amid the columns. You wake up from a dream in which you and Cass are walking into the ocean. You wake up again, mid-scream like every other show day because of all that could go wrong, and that in itself is a comfort — the possibility of regular failure is a comfort.

Even with the bridges closed, the house is nearly full. There are parents in the audience, colleagues, friends, cousins. Even if we don't know them, even if our parents and friends and cousins have evacuated, they are ours tonight.

There is no one to give the pre-show speech, so Antigone has to. You step up. You feel eyes on you from the sound booth. You try to make it sound like less of an indictment:
The State of California.
There are guards on the bridges.
Would like me to remind you.
Sirens at all hours, on all streets.
That in the unlikely event
The hospitals are overrun.
Of an emergency,
Smoke closer and closer every single day.
The exit is
Next to the sound and light booth
There.
The green EXIT sign flickers. You feel the whoosh of smoky night air from outside as the stage door is closed. You smell Ismene's last cigarette. Even inside, the air is buried. You hear the ghost light and mystery fan turning on, as if for you.

When you step back out, you're Antigone. Grief is not a costume. It's the first letter of your found name.

Creon announces his decree. He gives it all the love and hurt and disappointment he's carried these last few months. He gives it to his daughter, his lovers, and you, and he turns away from you before he's done, because he knows you can't save anyone from themselves.

Ismene runs to you and tells you to give it up, let Polyneices go unburied, walk away, let things get better. Save yourself, sister. But now, from here, you know she's wrong, and you're no one's sister.

Haemon, for all his strength, can do nothing to protect you. There is no fitness training to prepare us for this day.

We had plenty of warning. Thebes is a burnt landscape we failed together. You turn to Polyneices. You bury him lovingly up to his neck.

Polyneices keeps coughing.

Of course all the warnings were never enough for you (don't fall in love, don't share this mortality, don't bury the boy), and all the signs were never enough. We thought: not us. Not me. Not this city. We thought, *just one more day.*

Creon must have opened a palace window. It's hot. You wait for the chorus lights to flicker.

But now Ismene screams, and exits the wrong way, into the audience.

Because something isn't right.

Something backstage is off.

The Stage Manager in you is angry at the mistake before you realize what it is, that smoke is coming from behind the palace.

A firebird spark flies into the dark theater. The audience makes a collective sound. And now the stage itself is on fire. The Sphinx is burning. And just like that, you're off script. You watch it travel, the fire, now wild, not contained in stoves or campsites or lighters.

6. Intermission

The day after the sand arrived, we had the rehearsal where every-one laughs and everyone breaks character and it's a riot. We knew the lines too well and it was all an absurdity. *My brother's dead, bummer. Guess I gotta bury him,* said Jessica/Antigone. Haemon grabbed Polyneices' ankles and wheelbarrowed him around the stage. *Where shall we bury him? How about here? Here's nice!* While Creon followed around, *I forbid it! The curtains don't match! Not at this angle, are you mad?* Polyneices was choking on his laughter and sand, mouth open, trying to breathe, and Cass threw on disco lights. We buried Polyneices together up to his neck for the first time. He couldn't get out by himself. We tickled his nose and he pleaded for mercy, laughing. We threatened to leave him there, walking out, but we loved one another so much back then, we barely let a second go by before we rushed back in and hugged him and lifted him out of the sand together and high above our heads.

7. Antigone

The audience stands, but no applause comes.

It's a real tragedy, what could have happened next.

This was our pretend house, the way it used to be: sticky floors, dusty walls, broken ceiling fan. We built worlds here, but not like this: audience standing up, a man and a woman dressed in blue stumbling the wrong way, the sound booth illuminated from the wrong side with light Cass can't soften.

It would have been terrible to let it play out this way: Creon running for the exits, helping a man with a walker, you wondering what was on his mind that he had so much to live for but could not let one person go; Ismene stepping over her robes and heels, falling down, getting up, elbowing someone in the ribs, precisely, but then turning back to drag them along and dropping them halfway. Haemon pulling the door open so fast, hitting a young boy in the face, the boy falling, Haemon trying to pull him back. Polyneices yelling from the sandpit, stuck, and Sound & Lights in the booth, which the fire might have already taken. The Exit sign shorting and flashing off, with no time for metaphor or catharsis. Exit. Sound Booth. Polyneices. Exit. Sound booth.

It wouldn't have been a success because there would have been no good options. It's not a good tragedy if there is nothing to learn from it, other than the fact that fire burns.

8. Adaptation

It would all be different with spiders.

The front row is on fire. The people at the exit are pounding the door.

Spiders are so much scarier than fire in a theater: eight legs, eight eyes, some that only see light. Spiders suspend from the ceiling instead of hanging themselves dead for an abstraction like *honor*.

People trying to get the hell out of Thebes. The pillars of the styrofoam civilization lighting up like a torch, bright orange.

It's the best idea for an adaptation.

The door of the sound booth stuck. Polyneices buried.

In this version, the stage will be completely razed, nothing left but sand, and everyone will be a spider. Antigone, a Minax; Creon, a wolf spider; Polyneices in his polo and khakis, a carpenter; Ismene, a tarantula. We'll have to get a dramaturg. Or maybe an arachnologist. We'll have to find out what spiders do with their dead. The audience will go wild.

Listen, we'll say, listen. Dead people forgive. Everyone forgives eventually. Listen, we'll say, you can always become anything you want, all you ever needed was people to see you. The rest is adaptation.

Already your body is transforming, evolving slowly, but faster and faster, and you come down, undangling, touching the stage, eight ways.

In this version, we'll forget the lines. Antigone will walk across the stage roping everyone into the same story, first Polyneices, then Creon, then Haemon and Ismene, the director, the crew. That's one way it could go. We'll weave everyone into this web so that if/when one of us falls, we'll all feel it, everyone ritually tied, no one ever getting away, getting hurt.

Polyneices is fighting the sand. The sound booth is across the stage.

~~You~~ I easily find the shape of a creature that weaves shapes to survive.

You feel the ~~heat~~ strength of the ~~fire~~ web in your hands.

For a second, you have all of them in your story web: Creon, fighting through the lobby, Haemon, grabbing the boy's feet and pulling him out, Ismene and her handbag, Cass, grateful and easily extracted from the booth, and all that is left to do is build a silky bridge across a doorway and swing for the ocean.

And then the ghost light burns out and we're in the dark for what feels like a long time. There is banging outside. Something collapses. There is no more exit row.

The next time we come here, we will count the burned chairs. We will carefully test out the part of the stage that is still standing, see if it can hold us. We will say, Hamlet, but after a big fire. Cherry Orchard, but backwards. Tempest, but dry. For now, it's enough that we have Thebes. You taste the ground through each of your eight feet, yellow sand, red sun, blue sky, red blood. You pull and pull at the sand while Polyneices struggles to help. Must have been a beautiful place, Thebes. Finest sand in the world. Sand like a beach not too far from the water. Imagine it opening and tumbling all of us out to sea.

Note posted on lamp post near Market and Thare

IV. ~~Tales of Hope~~
Tales of Post Memory

Seb,
Writing fast, hope you see
this.

Fire on our old block.
Streets are full of smoke. I'm
here helping.

Lost: No Exit Theater, the
Expresso, The Paradise, all
gone.

Take Care
Please be safe,
J.

Jay,
Where are you?

When I woke up I looked out
the window and thought:
Snow! Then the smoke hit my
lungs.

The night sky is full of ash. I
was out looking for you.
Someone ran into me hard.

Made it to B. Collective
If you get this, come find me.
S.

S,
More fires in other buildings.
Just burning between
concrete.

If you get this please tell me
you're safe.
J.

S,
We pulled Cass out of the
rubble an hour ago.

Cass bled all over my hoodie.
Her leg is bad, but she'll be
ok.

The smoke cleared. So many
of us were out here, hauling
rocks. Funny community,
always so mad at each other
until there's an apocalypse.

*Remember the night we saw
stars? We were on the roof.
There was wind. Probably
someone else's hurricane, but
on that night it pushed the
smog away. And we saw —*

So many people we shared
these spaces with. Remember
K, your little dalliance? They
shared their water with me.
To think I was so mad when
you kissed them.

*The sky was full of stars, like a
great ocean of new fish, new
stories, and you said —*

I wish we could all just sail
away together.

Did we really see stars?

Cakes didn't make it.
This is what happens when
you hold on.
Hope glimmers and
glimmers and then
everything burns down.

*If I were brave, I'd go find out
with you.*

And you know what else? My
coat was on my chair at the
theater. And my Exodus 3
ticket was in it. Burned. I
guess you have your wish
now. Congratulations.

*Why am I asking you to
remember? You don't
remember anything. Fine. Go.*

We found the painted sign
that used to hang above The
Paradise.
It's broken in half. I pulled it
out for you.
J.

*We all heard about your ticket.
I'd give you mine if I could. S.*

~~The Little Match Girl~~
Five is the Other Shade of Red

This is how you tell a story: you set up the stakes, deliver the complications, palm the missing piece, and subvert the expectations at the end. It's a simple formula: do these things, and everyone comes away satisfied. Paint into the right squares, you'll have a picture you can frame.

The story is about the last night we were all together. The setting is a queer bar that is now gone. The missing piece is Anna, AnnA-Coming-Or-Going, who could have been the love of my life. The reveal is that she can never be found. Knowing that, there should be no reason to go on. Right?

❦

On Sunday, Jacks-the-roommate comes home with a box. On the cover of the box is a picture of Monet's *Water Lilies*, or rather, half of Monet's *Lilies*, the other half a grid of swirling shapes, each with a little number in the corner.

"No thanks," I say, from deep within a pile of blankets.

"Thought you'd like it," Jacks grins.

True that I always worry I got into art school by accident. True that because I don't know the minimum — not composition, not color, not who's Rembrandt — my non-working Sundays are for trying to paint. But not like this. Not with a paint-by-numbers set, with my heart in unnumbered pieces.

I like Jacks, with her Mick Jagger mouth and her overalls and her little neon ceramic genitals that hang all over our walls and in galleries across town. I like how she puts the box down on the coffee table and then picks it back up and pops it back at me, hyperextending her elbows, *here!*

"You could use a creative outlet."

"It's just a breakup," I say, "hearts grow back," hating the little sob that comes.

But that's when Jacks asks: "What breakup?"

Outside, generic morning birdsong.

"I told you. Anna broke up with me." It's hard to get these words out.

"Who's Anna?"

It takes me a minute. I'm slow like that.

"You're right," I say, "Ha, ha, who even *is* Anna?" I try a smile.

Jacks blinks at me slowly, tan skin with a natural glow, striking blue eyes she's tired of explaining or receiving compliments on.

"No. I mean … what?"

"Friday night." I remind her. "At the bar. We went out to The Paradise."

"I wish." Jacks says. "We went to Big 8. We played pool."

"We went to The Paradise," I repeat, patiently. "We danced. You said, *we deserve a gay night.*"

"Honey —" It's bad when Jacks starts with *honey.* "The Paradise has been closed for years. Now it's donuts. You ok? You fell pretty hard."

You're messing with me, I think. Ok, I'll play. "What do you remember about Friday?"

"I told you. We got drunk. You fell. You're probably still hungover. Maybe you have a concussion. You're moping. So *here*." The box. The lilies.

The front door is wide open, letting in cold air from outside, the stoop, the clean street, the electric train, the green rooftops and solar panels, the trees, the branches on the trees, the too-many leaves, and the wind; this wind, it swirls into the corners of the room, hollowing out the spaces between bones, pulling everything apart, tables, chairs, desk separating, sliding across the floor screaming, and here are the books flying off the shelves, the carpet rolling over and over itself, spiraling outward.

"You ok?" Jacks asks, concerned. "What's wrong?"

"Nothing. Shut the door." Please.

She does.

The ground rights itself and the furniture slides back into place, including that beige faux leather couch, but unconvincingly, like they'll start up again the minute I stop watching. *Fuck you. I see you.*

"Huh?" says Jacks.

"Nothing." I pull out my phone and turn it on.

And I exhale, relieved, furious, relieved.

There we all are in the picture: me, Jacks, Gay Ali, but not his twin Straight-ish Alex. Alex is in the mountains on a residency we're all jealous of, especially since his art is just so damn hetero, and here is Anna in the back, her bright red hair, her pale arm standing out against my shoulders, her green eyes.

We're standing outside a red painted sign that says Paradise with a heart over the i. Against the brick wall of the historic bar, you can see the outline of the bartender taking the picture, a bartender we love, a hard femme with spiky hair who can't even take a picture straight, and we're all sweating because it's been unseasonably hot, but we don't care. After that photo, we went back inside.

We drank, danced, and later Anna texted me, *it's over*, but in that photo we were happy.

"Jacks?"

I hand her the phone. She looks at it and smiles. She hands it back to me.

"I think the only one drunker than you was Alex."

"That's not Alex, that's Ali."

"Definitely Alex, look at his tattoo." I lean over. She's right. In the photo is Alex, the straight twin, with his anchor tattoo he got after drinking a bottle of rum. And I am looking at a completely different picture.

In this picture, we're in front of a bar with big wide windows and TVs showing every shade of sports. The bar is crowded. The neon is bouncing a shadow off the photographer, a wide-shouldered guy, his legs spread wide, a bar towel at his belt giving him a tail like a bull. There is no Anna, only me, Jacks, and Alex with his stupid tattoo.

My head starts rattling the furniture again.

"You're right," I say, slowly. "You're right."

"Get some rest," she says. "Don't make me worry." As she walks away, I hear her snort, "Paradise," like it's a TV show for children she hasn't thought of in years.

After her door shuts, I scroll through my pictures. No Anna. No mention of The Paradise. I drag my blanket to the window and look out at the blue skies, the cascade of native plants separating the sidewalk from the electric tramline. I count five butterflies. There's a rabbit nibbling at the dandelions. I almost smile, but I can't let go of this feeling, like a gas stove clicking, no spark, which is ridiculous. No one has a gas stove. I go back to my text messages. No Anna. No trace of our messages. I find only texts with Jacks and Alex about shopping, school, art shows, inside jokes, things I remember once I read about them, except the memories feel shallow, like they were just placed in a shop window for me to see.

Maybe when my head clears I'll know what to do.

I open the paint-by-numbers box. I take out the colors and the canvas, empty but jumbled with lines and numbers where the paint should go.

It's no fun, art. Mostly, it's walking to a dry place that was supposed to be an underwater paradise and staring at all the fossilized fish. Once or twice, if you're lucky, you can walk through a marble arch and find the ocean. I'm afraid of that ocean, with its jagged edges and currents. I love that ocean. Today, painting is just a desert and me praying to find a dusty plastic bottle with a drop of saltwater inside. I open the first tub of paint.

1. One is Red, Which is Expected

#1 is Red. There are a lot of 1s on the canvas. I don't remember so much red in *Lilies*, but I get started anyway.

The first vibrant red was Crimson Lake. It was made, is made, from the crushing of unimaginable numbers of cochineal insects. You gather them by the millions, still alive, and smash them to make red things — carnations, kings, madonnas, the blood of Jesus, candy you eat at the movies.

The following things are also red: the inside of The Paradise, the barstools covered in red velvet. The walls, the painted sign. The words on the flyers, "Organize To Stop the Pipeline," Anna's lips.

I love this bar. I love the feel of the curved wood bartop. I love that it's just a narrow strip with barely enough space to walk behind the barstools without brushing up against beautiful strangers, and then a space that should be too small for dancing, and then three bathrooms. I love the name, honoring Paradise

DeVine, who refused to stop singing when they came to shut it down, a microphone in one hand and a brick in the other.

This night at The Paradise, we were drinking red wine, and Anna got up and smiled at me. She walked past all of us towards the bathrooms. She texted: "find me."

I thought I might frame that text, send it to the Louvre. I squeezed Ali's shoulder as I passed. Jacks raised her glass to me, a toast.

The Paradise has three bathrooms all painted red, each with a urinal and a toilet. The bathroom on the far left has been out of order for a long time, both the urinal and the toilet smashed by a ceiling vent that came down in an earthquake years ago. The one on the far right is the one with the fire exit. Back in the evil days of raids, when the bar had a different name (Harry's or Henry's) this is how we'd get out, pushing our most vulnerable out first, feathers snagging on the door hinges. The stall in the middle has the only mirror.

I looked at all three doors. I smiled. I prayed. I chose the one on the left.

Anna was there. She leaned against the sink. I kissed her amid the graffiti and I cut my forearm on a sharp porcelain edge, but never felt it because of Anna's lips, the wine on her breath, that room, its perfect red.

❧

"How are those water lilies?" Jacks asks, holding a six-pack of honeyberry flavored soda.

"Great," I say, turning my canvas away.

I pull up my sleeve. There is a raised scar where I cut my arm on the porcelain. When I look again, it's gone.

When you draw over the lines in paint-by-numbers, you feel a little resistance, like a door sticky from decades of paint.

"Find me," the text from Anna burns in my mind, like when you stare at the sun.

2. Two Is Orange, Which Is Not Blue

The second tub is orange. I also don't remember much orange in *Water Lilies*. Or maybe this is part of painting: you add complexity, like Anna's hand in mine, a beach with not too many dead fish washed up, a sky orange from fires, orange being a complement of blue.

There's no trace of orange in the perfect blue sky outside the kitchen window. Three bumblebees work the lavender. Jacks comes skipping out of her room in blue overall shorts hooked on one side. "Good work," she says approvingly. "Art makes life beautiful." She heads to the kitchen.

I try to make Monet's pond pleasant despite the orange, color of algae bloom, red tide, fire on an oil slick in the ocean, plastic chip bags, safety equipment, prison uniforms.

A phone rings. Jacks doesn't answer, busy with a picnic basket.

"You going to get that?"

"Nope," she sings.

"Who's calling?" The phone is still ringing.

"Probably just a scam."

I stand up and edge towards the phone. The name there — Anna? Alex? Something with an A?

"What's wrong?' She's out of the kitchen now.

"Can I see who it was?"

She unlocks her phone and shows me missed calls, all of them labeled "City Services."

"I'm going out for a bit," she says. "Will you be ok?" Shouldering the picnic basket, she exits into clear air and daisy-scented sun.

You can't have orange the color, of course, without violence: saffron, colonization of South Asia, the volcanic pigment Orpiment used both for medicine and for arrowheads, exploitation of citrus farmers, pesticides. You need orange juice for a tequila sunrise.

The Paradise is an old bar. The barstools are mostly broken, the pictures crooked on the wall. The wallpaper is beginning to peel off from the heat, showing the orange glue beneath. We were talking about the usual things: art fellowships, drought, galleries, fires, dating, pollution — Jacks, Gay Ali, the bartender, Anna and me. The sky was orange again. That week, they found the last shark in the Indian ocean washed up on a white sand beach. We were looking up whether sharks lay eggs when Ali threw down his phone and lurched back from it, like it was radioactive.

The land near his brother Alex's residency was on fire.

We crowded around him. Ali was leaning back, gripping the bar.

"Are you sure?" we said, "Let's see," we said, reaching for our own phones.

"They'll send helicopters."

"They'll beat back the fire."

The bartender said her ex was a firefighter, Alex would be fine. She made us all tequila sunrises. To distract Ali, we talked about hope: the water protectors fighting a new pipeline, people protecting the land for the 47th day now — one of Jacks's cousins was there, camping out, Ali was putting together supplies to send — the divers who blew up the Nord Stream pipeline decades ago, just a few people with diving suits and explosives, and everyone with a

PADI license taking note: we can unbuild these structures. It's possible.

"And if the fires come here?" Jacks asked.

"They won't," I said. "We're safe here."

Anna looked at me and stood up. I didn't feel her brush past as she walked by. I remember her perfect back, her strong shoulders and the roll of skin between her tank top and sports bra. I waited for her to text me. She didn't. I found her in the middle stall. She wouldn't look at me, except through the mirror.

"I don't think we're safe here," she said, "and if we are, we shouldn't be."

Now, in our apartment, with the blue sky outside, I look at the photo of Alex at The Big 8. I guess he was fine in the end, wasn't he? We're fine now. Outside the window it begins to rain gently. Jacks comes in and leans a blue umbrella against the yellow door jamb. Art.

There are so many things I want to know.

Do you remember when the air was smoky?

How did Alex escape the fires?

"Was the sky ever orange?" I ask.

"Why would the sky be orange?"

3. Three Is Green, Which is Envy

When I open paint tub #3, I decide they've given me the wrong box. How can this be *Water Lilies?* The green is a bright toxic "danger: radiation" kind of green. Did they update *Water Lilies* for climate change?

"Climate change?" Jacks laughs. "Here?"

I've already snapped at Jacks twice this morning, once over the teapot (she boils one cup at a time). "It's a waste of energy," I said. She just shrugged and said, "It grows on trees," pointing out the kitchen window at boxed plants with photosynthetic receptors. The second time I snapped was over her texting.

"Who are you texting now?" I asked, meaning *how can you text now?*

"Jealous?" she asked, which reminded me of Anna. *Don't be jealous*, she said, or *how can you be jealous?*

"I know you're having a hard time," Jacks says, "but you need to chill out." Behind her a bluebird hops around the windowsill. I watch her drink a full glass of water like it comes out of the tap.

"You're right,' I say.

She begins to cough. My heart races. She spits water into the sink. I realize nothing is wrong.

She's off to teach a pottery class, in jeans and an orange top, so bright. I hear her say good morning as she steps onto the electromagnetic tram. I pull the painting out.

I want to inhale the green. Color of lily pads, marshes, frogs, fronds, or maybe dollars.

The wallpaper at The Paradise had peeled off completely, framed posters leaving a green streak as they slid slowly down. Orange sky summer was over. Now all we talked about was green: a new kind of vine was creeping over our city, invasive, thorny, crumbling walls, thickening the air with pollen; the ocean was turning viscous and olive-colored, waves clinging to the shore like mold.

We were worried about life after art school and about the green mist that left piles of dead birds everywhere. The bartender was quiet, counting green cash at the bar quickly, right in front of us.

On the television behind the bar, a news anchor wearing a ponytail and pearls from the sea pursed her lips, pretending concern. *But only in some areas,* a reporter was saying, *mostly just—* and said the name of our county. The bartender punched the wall. We understood. We had never felt the hurt of that particular localization. *Residents are adapting,* the reporter said. The bartender curled over the bar, shoulders tight and shaking. Eventually, she went back to counting.

Let me make sure I understand, the news anchor said. *These are toxins from algae, like in water?*

The bartender stopped counting. "It's not going to be enough," she said. "It's too late."

What can you tell us about containment? said the news anchor. *I heard police …*

"It's not too late," Anna said. The bartender turned to look at us. When she did, I saw what had happened to one side of her face. It was yellow-green, like oxidized copper. The skin of her cheek was sagging at her cheekbone, and the skin on the bottom weighed down, already beginning to rip. It happened to a lot of people that summer who went into the ocean, despite the signs about algae blooms. It was beginning to happen to people who lived near the ocean. Ali had been coughing.

"I know someone who can help," Ali said. "We just need to get you out of the city." But when he opened his mouth to say "city," there was a soft sound. On the bar, on wood, was a tooth, pulled out at the roots, so clean. Anna put an arm around him at the same time as I found myself edging away.

You know what else is green? Radium. Picture workers, mostly women, painting it onto clocks and dying of exposure. Other greens include verdigris, copper cousin that settles in lungs and goes to your head, like jealousy; Scheele's green, containing arsenite, picture women in green dresses fainting; every bottle of poison in every cartoon, at least three gin bottles glowing on the shelf of the bar.

Ali was the first to take out his wallet and count out his remaining cash. Then Anna. Then Jacks. Last, me. We slid what we had over to the bartender who took it and thanked us.

"Don't show your face outside," Jacks whispered. She drew on a napkin a map to a safer place, out of the city. She barely had time to finish before blue and red lights flashed outside.

It was Anna who walked the bartender to the third stall and helped her to the exit. When I turned around, I saw the bartender, her arms around Anna's shoulders. Anna kissed the bartender's cheek, the side that was still whole.

So when I screamed at Anna later in the parking lot, it wasn't really about toxic algae.

"You don't even know her! You could've gotten sick."

She said I was jealous, and there was no room for jealousy at the end of the world.

"Then maybe I'm not good enough for the end of the world."

She said it mattered that we go down fighting.

"I don't want to fight." I said. "I want to live."

You know what else is green? Memories, corrosive and corroding like battery acid (often green). The more you visit them, the more the guardrails melt away.

⁂

Now, here with my paint-by-numbers kit, I paint another green shape.

"So why do you get to live?" Anna's voice. Clear as seaglass. Right behind me.

135

I'm on my feet. Gripping the couch. But there's no one here. Just me. Just my head.

I close my eyes. I count down from 10. Take a breath. 9. Nothing to see but dark. 8. I let my breath deepen. 7. In the dark behind my eyelids, a flash of green light. Green eyes. Anna's eyes. In the dark, in my memory, Anna's eyes open. I hear banging, the sound of someone trying to escape a small room. Louder and louder, the banging, as if the person were pounding on every available surface, then muffled yelling. I open my eyes. She's not there. But I swear I smell her minty perfume.

"This is a concussion," I repeat, over and over. The room is dark. "This is —"

A knock on the front door. From outside, from the street, green light casts out under the threshold.

"Jacks," I yell. "Jacks!"

"What do you want?" Jacks comes out in furry pajamas even though it's summer, air conditioning blasting from her room. She turns on so many lights.

I point at the door. Jacks opens it. There's nothing out there but a cool night breeze, the hooting of owls. "You're just tired," she says, handing me a mason jar full of water. "Go to bed."

In my head, as if muffled behind a door, I can almost remember the conversations we had, me and Jacks and Ali and Anna. The ceramicists at our school had walked out, led by Jacks, giving up clay to repair the water, putting on gloves and pulling algae. There were people helping immunocompromised friends out of the city.

"We have a chance to help," she said.

"I just got into art school," I said. What I meant was "why now, the end of the world? Why can't someone else save the world? Why me?" And we sat there, on her floor, her open bag next to me full of postcards and flyers and petitions and maps.

I close my eyes.

A bathroom stall. Blacklight. Graffiti. The sound of Anna's quickening breath. The graffiti changes. It says, *I love you.* It says, *Help.* It says, *It's over.* It says, *Find me.*

I wait until I hear Jacks snoring. I open another tub of paint.

4. Four is White, Which is Forgetting

This is how you tell a story. You get all the words out in front of you. Then you erase what doesn't belong.

White paint was made with lead, which absorbs through the skin into the bloodstream and bones. You get high blood pressure, you get *painter's colic,* a euphemism for erasure: melancholy, blindness, forgetting.

That winter, the streets around The Paradise were covered in white dust. I wasn't there much because I was painting. Painting was effortless back then. Anna and Ali were out, at city hall, in front of energy companies, blocking bridges. There was a billboard I remember passing on the way to my studio. It featured a smiling family in a white room with a door painted green. "Fracking for Life!" it said.

⸎

Now, here, I feel the ground shaking, my hand shaking, tiny drips of white scatter on the coffee table. I look up. "Jacks?" I call, but I know she's out. Her green-painted door is closed.

All is well. There is only our apartment, with the empty walls and beige accents and green door, all behaving. No dust.

I don't understand how a whole corner of the canvas now needs to be white but I begin anyway, obeying the #4 bubbles that begin to overlap the other colors, red, orange, green, erasing them.

"It's over," Anna texted me. "We're leaving. You could come." There were people assembling outside the city, coming together to stop excavations. "Come help us protect whatever water there is."

"My life is here," I said. I was working on my thesis: a giant landscape, done all in white. The school was still open. Classes were in session. "Maybe I'll come find you after graduation."

Jacks and I went to say goodbye to Anna and Ali at The Paradise. We drank the last of the well liquor because water was scarce. Anna and Ali huddled, whispering over a map.

"If we get separated, meet here."

"Don't stop for anyone."

"If you see a pool, drink, but not too much."

Anna looked tired that night, her red hair cut short. "Are there any pools left?"

I waited until the map was put away.

"Hey," I said. I don't know what I wanted to say, but I swear she was in the act of turning back to look at me.

Then the walls were shaking. Empty bottles clinking in the well. "Earthquake," Ali said.

"Obviously —" said Anna.

Then darkness. Then a terrible sound like the ground opening, probably the facade of the old building coming down. Hard things falling around us.

"Go," someone yelled, "back." We ran to the back of the bar while ceiling tiles came down. We stumbled in the dark, Ali, me, Anna, Jacks. Shaking. "Third bathroom," I said, and I turned around to grab Anna, and Anna tried to grab Jacks. There was kicking, and Anna's hand on my jacket, and Jacks would have reached for me, but I felt the clean air, pushed hard for it, and suddenly I was down the fire exit and outside with Jacks, coughing on dust.

I opened my eyes. *Take it all away*, I thought. A cloud of dust enveloped me, white on white, like my painting.

⁂

Gentle chimes wake me. I pull at my dream: me and Anna, before the earthquake, sitting in this room. "Stay with me." I said.

"It's over," she said. "I can't stay here."

"It's safe here."

Anna turned her eyes on me then. I saw her eyes flicker from pale jade to petroleum, flammable. "If you find a safe place," she said, "Find me."

I sit straight up.

I know where Anna is. Where she has been the whole time. I open the box, fingers shaking. There are four paint tubs here, but there are five numbers on the canvas: A fifth color.

5. Five is the Other Shade of Red

This time, I don't even call Jacks. I know that if I go into her room, there will be nothing there. Maybe a closet with two empty hangers rattling in the tremors of our shaking city.

The most poisonous color of all is the color you don't see, how octopodes become sand-colored to attack, how an eel can hide in the fold of a rock, how memory can render a person both alive and dead, how so much can be happening at the same time: an island of plastic, a covering of smog over a city, a river on fire, and we couldn't even see it from here.

When the front door doesn't open, I shove it hard with my shoulder. The birds are still singing, the exact same song. As I walk and then run down the cobbled, bike-path lined, green-rimmed street, the colors bleed. I see numbered ridges where the ground has been plumbed for oil.

As I run, I think of what Jacks said. *The Paradise, now it's donuts.* I let my feet guide me, coughing on the dry dust. I know where to go.

The store that sells overpriced donuts is painted gray with a giant donut mural. The glaze on the mural donut is sickeningly pink. A white man with oil slick hair smiles and lingers in the doorway, holding the door open for me. I am clutching my *Water Lilies*, in burnt orange, toxic green, blood red.

When I push past the man at the door, a little bell rings. Pretty people look up at me from stainless steel tables. I walk past the long shiny glass counter that used to be a bar. Here, it's bright and perfect and the coffee smells delicious and people are laughing.

The woman behind the counter has a name tag: "Daisy."

"How can I help you?" says Daisy. She smiles at me. Her lipstick is donut-frosting-pink, which must be required, because it doesn't suit her. Her eyes and smile glaze as I walk past her to the end of the store, where there are three bathrooms: women, men, employees.

I hesitate for a second. I try to call up that last night, its dust and screams. I choose the middle stall.

It's just a bathroom: white and pink tiles, a mirror, a little plug-in device with a light up donut that puffs out donut-scented air. I want to believe it's real.

I prop the painting on the mirror. I trace my fingers along the tiles to see if any of them have any give. Not this one. This one is perfect. Not that one. Nothing wrong, just perfectly straight tile. Maybe this *is* real. Maybe I could go home now, back to Jacks. I could say, "You were right, I was stupid." I could pick up another paint-by-number and try again. I could say, "Let's call Alex, go the Big 8."

But then I feel something. A give. This one. This tile is just a little softer.

I call up a memory of porcelain tiles cracking, the ceiling bowing. It looks like the grout on one edge of the tile wants to crumble. I scratch at it. It fritters. So I claw at it with my bitten-down nails. It fritters some more. I dig in now and my nail catches, skin tears. I keep going. Resisting. I manage to hook one finger behind the tile and pull. The air changes, thickens with smoke. The lights go out, all except for the little donut nightlight. I close my eyes and keep digging. Two tiles fall apart like a book, releasing a smell so full and rank, I have to step back.

Between the tiles, slowly, comes a thick snake. No. A thick pale arm with copper hair, and long fingers, silver ringed, that join mine in digging, and then fingers that grip mine so damn hard, and I grip back, and go back to digging, both hands.

The painting has fallen to the floor. I can't look at it head on now. It would be too much: the dead fish, the orange sky, the green corroding, the white bleached coral, a process so much bigger than us that we will never be able to fight or control. The water lilies are spattered in blood in an oil slick lake full of sludge, and there is no place for art in this world, unless I can go back there. Now the hole is big enough that I can use my arm. I keep pulling tiles. I brace my feet against the wall. Now Anna is pounding on the other side of a wall of a bathroom that has been razed, but lives in memory. We are breaking it down together, tile by tile.

This is how you tell a story: you tell it to yourself over and over until its pigments break down into colors you can see. Tell it right and something might reach back: the confident grip of an arm, the better version you could have been. Pull hard enough and maybe the bar will be there, just as it was: the red countertops, red barstools, the orange lights, orange bottles, the green of the exit sign, of grass, of Anna's eyes, all of it — the oil rigs and the chance we had to stop them.

When she comes out, I will face her, in her perfection: the raw red hairless patches on her scalp, the green bruising on her skin, the blood around her mouth, the green and orange of rot around cuts and burns that won't heal, the vines that wrap around her feet, the shifting surface of a face I still love so much. Together we will see to it that the bar is still there. We will draw as many maps as we need. She will take my hand in her softening grip.

"You were right," I'll say, "you were —"

Her kiss will taste like butterflies, weeds, algae, a pile of wet dry leaves in autumn, perfect.

"You're here," she will say, laughing and kissing me again. "We're here."

Community Count:
T-Minus 6
Lost: Dion, Mosh, Cakes, Sam, Aux
Tickets left: 10. Held for those wounded in *No Exit* fire.
We will be gathering Monday night to honor the lost.

At B. Collective
Please tell your friends

Jay!

I was at B. Collective helping out and I saw a spider. A real spider. Little. Black. 8 legs. It crawled out from the rubble by No Exit theater. I chased it. It skittered into the vine forest.

You know what that means? That means there are living things there. There's life in the vine forest!

You know who probably went into the forest? Dion. You know what they said? They had a ticket to sell. If a spider can live in the vines, maybe Dion can too. Maybe they still have their ticket. Maybe there are other things there: collectives, trees, Mosh, KC, birds?

If I brought you a spider, would you believe there's something to stay for? What if I found Dion and got you a ticket? What if I found the woods?

Wouldn't that be brave?

S.

Full Color Illustration

A little matchgirl lights a match and sees a vision of love.

Thank you to The Paradise. Thanks for your open floors, your tiny windows, your bulletin boards. Your terrible bathrooms. The Paradise was a place, and places are made up of people, and sometimes people go. We are gathered here today to say goodbye to Aux. Aux was with us since the 4 degree shift. They helped establish the first collectives: Octavia's, Harvey's, Audre's. They helped build the wheelchair accessible walkway across the Thare Street sinkhole. They connected us back to the state

[Audience reacts]

And I know not everyone liked that, but some of us needed access, and now we have options.

We are gathered here to say goodbye to Sam. I know a lot of you knew Sam. I know a lot of you knew Sam really well.

[Audience laughs]

Sam was the best of our organizers. They created the communication systems we use now. They plotted out our first carbon capture gardens. Thanks Sam. We love you.

We are gathered here to say goodbye to Cakes. Cakes ... Raise your hand if Cakes ever gave you free food, scowling at you the whole time. Don't be mad, Cakes, but we love you.

I guess Seb couldn't make it, but if they were here, they'd say that Cakes, Sam, and Aux are your stories to tell now.

Exodus 3 leaves in five days, but as we all learned last night, goodbyes aren't always on a schedule. Many of us will be gone. Many of us are still missing from last night.

I invite you to look around at all of us, gathered here. If the person next to you consents, maybe you put your arm around their shoulder.

Whatever happens next, we are here together now.

And that's something.

Dear Seb,

I should have known you wouldn't be at the memorial. You're never there when it counts.

Jay

V. ~~Tales of The Woods~~
Tales of The Creeping Vines

Jay-Jay My Friend —

Thanks for all you did the day of the fire — you saved our Comrade Cass.

We'd like to thank you by offering you a ticket to Exodus 3.

Big decision, right? — Throw your hope into what's left here, with the fires and the floods vs. risk the complete unknown — Flip it: risk the complete unknown of here — the vines, the cats, the fires, and whatever's next vs. throw your hope into humanity, that we'll be better somewhere else — Insh'Allah.

You have the honor of our last ticket — Last 10 tickets went to Cass and those of us with limited mobility and more access needs. They need the medical facilities on the ship. We need their collective care leadership on the new planet. Know what I'm saying?

You got Cakes' ticket. Rest in power, Cakes.

To answer your questions: Yes, the tickets are real.

No, I can't tell you how we got them — let's just say RG talked to the ship. Leave it at that.

Burn this. B. Collective doesn't archive.

Love & Disturbance

Ali

You know there's plants that only grow after catastrophes? Ruderal. Look it up.

POST CARD

from Exodus 2

COMMUNICATION — ADDRESS ONLY

Transcribed from Radio Signals by B. Collective

TRANSMISSION CORRUPTED

We've arrived on ____, and we are ____
The ocean is ____.
At night, the ____ ____ in the ____ and we ____

Wish you were here.

From Maxxy at Now Collective
to Cass at B. Collective

Ecstasy …

Never do that to me again. I can't believe we almost lost you. I won't think about it.

I know why you haven't written by the way. It's ok. We don't need to talk about it.

Here's a story to distract you; a new episode in the Ballad of Seb and Jay …

Ali and I were at B. listening to the transmission from Galactic Exodus 2. It was like getting a message from the ocean.

Seb was leaning against the wall scribbling in their book. They looked up at the old Paradise and wiped away a tear. I remember this moment so clearly. I could feel in my chest that something was going to happen. But they just looked at the ground, stared for a while. And then they took off into the vine forest.

An hour later Jay came running up, all: "Where's Seb?" Picture them: sleeveless, muscles, a sheen of sweat. When Ali pointed to the tangle of vines that used to be at least a few blocks away, but that was now just across the street already growing over the burned out buildings like Birnam Wood, Jay never hesitated. They grabbed the first thing they could find in their backpack, their hoodie left over from the day of the fire rescue, and threw it on for protection. Then Jay ran into the forest of vines wearing the hoodie stained red with your blood!

You see Earth continues to be lively. Don't be jealous!

That's right, Starlight … I know you're going on the ship. I'm not mad at you.

Ali and I finished transcribing the message from Exodus 2. They're alive but the adjectives are missing. All we got was a madlib we have to fill out for ourselves.

Let me try …

On New Earth, the sky is light purple and the surface of the water is bioluminescent. All the leaves are hollow so every wind plays a little song. Tiny birds drink salt water instead of nectar, and they sit around waiting to see if you're going to cry. Don't feed the alien hummingbirds, dear friend.

I have news of my own. Last night, I was walking home from Ali's (ask me no questions, I'll tell you no lies). I turned a corner and right there was a giant cat. This one was gray. Cass, I was so scared. It was huge. Face as big as a bus wheel. Bigger. I thought I was dead! I closed my eyes … When I opened my eyes, I was still alive. And it was gone …

I've decided you and I are both on the same adventure, even if they happen in different places. Like in elementary school when your teacher told you about geometry. Some lines cross and never meet again, some lines are side by side forever across space.

Miss you already.

Maxxy

INVITATION
THE INAUGURATION
OF THE
NEW PARADISE
200 FT. EAST OF
THE THARE STREET
SINKHOLE.
Exodus 3 Tickets Left: 0
We are locked in, folks.

Dear Jay, Who Was Right About Me All Along

I thought I could find you a ticket. Or at least something worth making you stay, like Dion, or a spider, or an olive branch.

Now there's vines in front of me. Vines behind me. So thick I can't move. Hurts to touch them. No way out. How will I ever get out of this hyperallergenic labyrinth?

They're cute, the vines that want to kill me. Almost green. Hard like cables. In some places their skin splits showing different filaments all wrapped around one another: plant matter, plastic, cables, something sticky and red I hope isn't muscle. Their smell is like a night at the bar: sweat and carbon and freshness and copper, sexy.

Just a quick break. In a minute I'll get up. I'll find my way back.

I'll tell you you were right.

I wanted you as a memory of what I survived — orange sky, ocean death, 4 degree shift, pandemic, other pandemic, the giant sinkhole, seeing you across the room and you turning away from me.

I'll tell you instead that there are always new woods to find. You don't even have to remember these.

When I get up. In a minute. That's when.

S

PS: Starting feel funy.

Time 4 last story?

This one's YRs.

Member day you jumped to hole? Sinkhole on Thare St.

And I cry?

Did not tell U ending: U hit YR head. I jumped in

Rescue U.

BCU made me brave.

Ha fun w starz

    S.

~~Little Red Riding Hood~~
Root Systems

TRANSMISSION: ENTER VINE FOREST; ENTER US, ONE (1) RED RIDING HOOD.
TRANSMISSION: Received.

Red Riding Hood enters the forest where Grandmother entered before, but does not leave.

TRANSMISSION: Lost.

TRANSMISSION: A crow flies above the canopy, lifted in its wings. The forest is shaped like the dot of a green question mark.
And beyond?
TRANSMISSION: Signal lost.
Why?
Where did Red Riding Hood go?

TRANSMISSION TO: FOREST EYES THAT LOOK AND DON'T BLINK
QUESTION: What was she wearing?

RETURN TRANSMISSION: *WHAT WAS SHE WEARING, THO?*
>Red Riding Hood is a girl wearing a provocative
>cloak = Danger
>Red Riding Hood is a boy wearing a hoodie =
>Danger
>Red Riding Hood was neither; in fact, the first
>time they put on the red riding hood was the
>first time they knew an answer to this question,
>*What are you?* In the folds of that red hood —
>>TRANSMISSION: Received.
>>ANSWER: I am Red Riding Hood.
>You need this type of *I* to do things, like enter the woods.
>>And get lost.

TRANSMISSION: A crow flies above the question of the forest. The air that spins around the trees captures the smell of a squirrel not alive but alive inside with bugs. The scent circles up, catches the crow. Crow dives.

TRANSMISSION: When a bird flies, is the flight in the feathers or in the bird? This is a trick question. Distracts the crow from the bigger question: hawk approaching, compressing air.

>Where go the crow?
>>The crow falls, is eaten.
>>>The crow falls, is eaten.
>>>>Some of the crow hits the ground
>>>>— two wings; loam, redwood pine
>>>>— and sinks slowly.
>>>>>Decomposition.

TRANSMISSION. TRANSMISSION. TRANSMISSION: A crow flies and flies above a green forest that is not there anymore, no more than the crow is there.
    The crow and the forest are
        down here in transmission.

TRANSMISSION: The crow fell and the forest ended.
QUESTION: Why did the forest end?
    TRANSMISSION: [Cut. Not received.]
    TRANSMISSION: A lumberjack cuts trees, cuts root systems, cuts lines.

TRANSMISSION: Around the crow there is now wolf.
    What's the deal with this wolf?
    TRANSMISSION: The wolf ate only one wing. He should have eaten two.
    Longing for flight with one wing. That's the
    kind of thing that makes fairy-tale wolves cruel.

ROOT INTERSECTION: UNDER THE OUTHOUSE BEHIND
GRANDMA'S HOUSE: SO MANY TRANSMISSIONS!

The lumberjack destroyed the forest.

Grandma and the lumberjack are having tea.
    Their stories first crossed at the
    root systems under Grandma's
    outhouse. He was trespassing. She
    was generous. It was embarrassing.
    Now they have tea every Thursday.

The lumberjack carries in his heart the spit of his father (also a lumberjack) because: splinters.

After tea, the lumberjack goes out back. To chop some wood, he says. But really to use the outhouse, with its sunken-in roof open to the canopy and the stars.

TRANSMISSION: BRIGHTNESS OF STARS: COOKIES: COMPOST: DECOMPOSITION

And she, grandmother, crosses the kitchen and puts on his lumberjack flannel, compressing her soft arms into the sleeves, and the smell of sweat and wood shavings (TRANSMISSION). She looks in the mirror, she likes what she sees — the way her short white hair now stands up, the way the shape of her two breasts in flannel now says something different than Forgotten&Neglected
TRANSMISSION: Take That&Fuck You
Grandma pushes her legs out and sticks her thumbs into the waistband of her gray pajamas and scowls at her reflection. She takes a fork, and now it's a cigarette, and she props one foot against the wall behind her, which is where the lumberjack finds her, walking through the door, he buckling up his pants, she smoking the cigarette-fork.

"I'll trade you for a day," is the lumberjack's transmission.

TRANSMISSION, FROM: TERMITE IN THE DOORJAMB: The lumberjack is thinking how nice it would be to stay here in the kitchen and bake. He puts on the apron.
Grandmother walks out the back door and picks up the ax.

When Red Riding Hood first saw the wolf, it was standing up against a tree, taking a piss.

> TRANSMISSION: FROM: WET SPATTERED
> LICHEN: Can you relate to a wolf with love?
> Probably not. Probably just envy. Or desire.

Lichen lives 3,600 years. Lichen remembers where Grandma first entered the forest.

TRANSMISSION: BONES OF RED'S GREAT GRANDMOTHER (TO RED'S GRANDMOTHER)

> Go visit your grandmother; see if she's dead yet.
> Here, might as well bring her something. Butter.
> What do you mean, how will you know?
> She's your grandma. She looks like you. Stubborn.

TRANSMISSION: REPEATED THROUGH TIME, IN AIR POCKETS IN THE SOIL, OVER AND OVER:

> Stay on the path.
> Stay on the path.
> Little Red Riding Hoods are always told to stay
> on the path.

ROOT ENDING:

> Grandma's house is a good place to hide from wolves?
> FALSE.
> For starters, there is no direct path there. You have to get there the long way.
> TRANSMISSION: Redirected.

Unlike wolves and Red Riding Hoods, trees support one another, undersoil collectives transmitting.

TRANSMISSION: End. Grandma-Lumberjack destroys the tree.
      QUESTION: Is the ax part of the forest for its wood handle?
TRANSMISSION: Here comes the wolf.

TRANSMISSION: A wolf crosses out of the forest, over a threshold.
            In the house, the wolf eats twelve dozen cookies
            and also eats Lumberjack-Grandma
            while Grandma-Lumberjack is destroying
            transmissions outside.

TRANSMISSION: PAGE FROM A STORYBOOK NOT YET
DECOMPOSED
            [[The very wicked wolf took a terrible leap into
            grandma's closet]]

GRANDMA'S CUTTING TRANSMISSION: Do trees fear death?
            ANSWER: Death is like a red hood is like
            performing Lumberjack is like time: only a
            growth ring.
            SO THEN: Not Grandma eaten by the wolf,
            but: lumberjack wearing Grandma's apron
            wearing the wolf as outer-skin. For a long time,
            s/he lived in the belly of a wolf, like we all do,
            for a time.

For a time, Lumberjack-Grandma wore the wolfskin and s/he survived, becoming Lumberjack-Grandma-Wolf, the same way that this person had to be eaten by the red riding hood becoming Red Riding Hood, to enter the woods.

TRANSMISSION, FROM: HOUSE MOLD: Now Here is Lumber-jack in grandma-drag in wolf in Grandma Lumberjack's underwear waiting for Red Riding Hood.

QUESTION: How did we get here?
  RESPONSE: Picture an old lady's underwear,
  but not like you think, not cotton sails. Nice
  underwear that still gives space for a grandma-
  style body. Lace, yes. But also elastic and blue
  tint from the towels in the wash.

The wolf (now lumberjackgrandmawolf) found grandma's (now Grandma-Lumberjack's) underwear, and it felt something. Wolf tested the elastic. Wolf had never thought about underwear, but it put four (4) paws in, two in each pant hole, and for the first time, it walked on all fours. It looked in the mirror and felt some-thing, a *he*-ness. The wolf saw himself looking soft and wild, which made him long for soft things, like a bed.

TRANSMISSION, FROM: BED BUGS: Enter Red Riding Hood. Late.
  Retreat.
  Root Ending:
  False Beginning.
  Do not begin the formula. There is only one way you can go once you initiate this transmission.
  TRANSMISSION: (You always begin anyway.)
    What big arms you have.
      What big eyes you have.
        What big legs you have.
  Stop.

QUESTION: What does it smell like inside an
apron inside a wolf inside a grandma's house
inside the woods?
Dinner. My what sharp teeth.
Consumption. Decomposition. Transmission.

QUESTION: How does program end?

RESPONSE: It ends with everyone dead and the
forest burned to the ground by wildfires, burned
to nothing, and below nothing, we survive.

QUESTION: We want to know about before.

Grandma-Lumberjack lovingly c-sectioned
them out, and they all came rolling into the sun
OR
Grandma-Lumberjack cut open lumberjack
dressed as wolf dressed as grandma and out
rolled Red.
OR
Lumberjack cut open wolf and out came
Grandma in red lingerie.
All are technically correct
transmissions.

SO IS THIS ONE: On another side of the forest live the wolves.
They re-enter the forest. They never encounter a human. They live
happily ever after.

The wolfskin is cut open. A fire inside. A campfire inside. A forest fire inside that reaches out and tears the whole forest down, the way grandmothers/lumberjacks always do if you let them.

> A burl full of seeds; a book.
> New story.
> A single drop of blood.
> New story.

TRANSMISSION: Red Riding Hood decomposing, remembers Red Riding Hood newly released to the sun, and wonders out loud:
> *¿If the wolf is my mother and lumberjack grandma*
> *is my sister and grandma lumberjack is my*
> *midwife, which is my true grandmother?*

Because Red's eyes once looked out the window at Grandma in her burgundy lumberjack flannel and lace underwear, therefore in these eyes there is still the image of Grandma cursing and cutting wood.
> TRANSMISSION = QUESTION
> But we know.

TRANSMISSION: THE GRANDMOTHER IS THE STORY IS THE FOREST IS THE TRANSMISSION:

We turn the crow's wing page: Transmission.

The story travels and continues, the way light moves across the trees in the eye of a crow that flies and is eaten, and we separate and synthesize and re-member, across transmissions, across time, and you, in your time, you keep on creating and recreating your selves and one another, over and over again in your stories. Just like us.

Dear Seb,

You are, as always, so fucking dramatic. Did you ever think of crawling out instead of writing a note?

First, you have no idea what I had to do to find you in those vines. Not to mention find the book you threw over your shoulder like a diva. I had to wrestle the book out of the vine that was wrapped around it. They grow so fast.

Second, you are and were always the one stomping away. You left me so many times before I finally had enough: for a book, a spider, a story, a view of stars. The apocalypse is like you — never a single ending: the oceans rising, the rearranging, the big wave, the one with the vines, the one with the falling birds, the one with a million tiny fights about nothing.

It's not your fault. Maybe it's not that you're dramatic. It's not that you like books more than people, or that you'd make out with a street sign if it stood in your way, or that you lack survival skills. There are a million survival skills and you know it.

It's because of the time I woke up and you were crying at the sunrise, both at the colors and at the pollution that made the sky iridescent, and the time I woke up and you were asleep drooling into a book about the woods, and the time we saw Exodus 1 explode and you wanted it to be stars.

All those times you were exactly where you were supposed to be. I wasn't. Even asleep in the woods with a book of stories in your hands, you are infuriatingly you.

When I pulled the vines off you, I realized they don't hurt me. They remind me of something from your stories. Something about the way they grow in disturbed soil. Something about the way they breathe, how they climb almost to the stars. They remind me of — I don't know.

Rest up. I'll see you at New Paradise. Maybe I'll let you ambush me for one last dance.

We take care of each other,

Jay

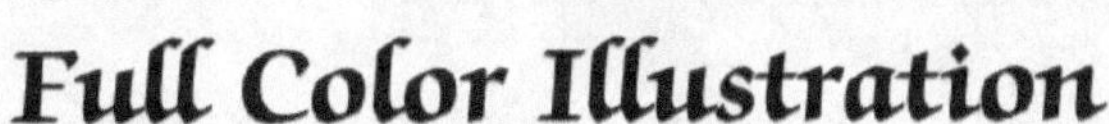

Full Color Illustration

Red Riding Hood Speaks to the Wolf; Two Paths Lie Before Her

CURRENT count, going from our little circle: Jay, Cass, Oli, K.

Staying: Seb, Ays, RG, Maxxy (me).

INAUGURATION of the New Paradise, written by Maxxy

T-minus-3

Tickets are gone.

We're all getting ready for some out-of-this-world FOMO.

They found a place for New Paradise, a building behind B. Collective that wasn't burned or flooded. It used to be one of those DNA labs, and it's still standing and that's about all you can say for it. We kept the name, after an activist from before the 4 degree shift who fought for our space. Because even if we're not there, we need to remember those who came before us.

They painted the name Paradise on a reasonably white sheet and hung it from the wall while the old sign we glued together dries. There's no door yet. We climb in through the window.

Which is how we saw them, Jay and Seb coming out of the vines. Jay looked like the toughest queer you've ever seen, hair you just can't cut badly spiking up with dirt and sweat, hoodie artfully torn showing collarbones, cheekbones of heartbreak, dust kicking up around them. And over their shoulder, Seb, face puffed red and wheezing but still cute.

The vines seemed to follow them, already trying to burst in, growing over everything. I say let them.

It's no enchanted castle, this, but it's ours. And someone is already pounding the ground to see if it wants to be a dance floor.

VI. ~~Tales of the End of the World~~ Tales of the World That Doesn't End

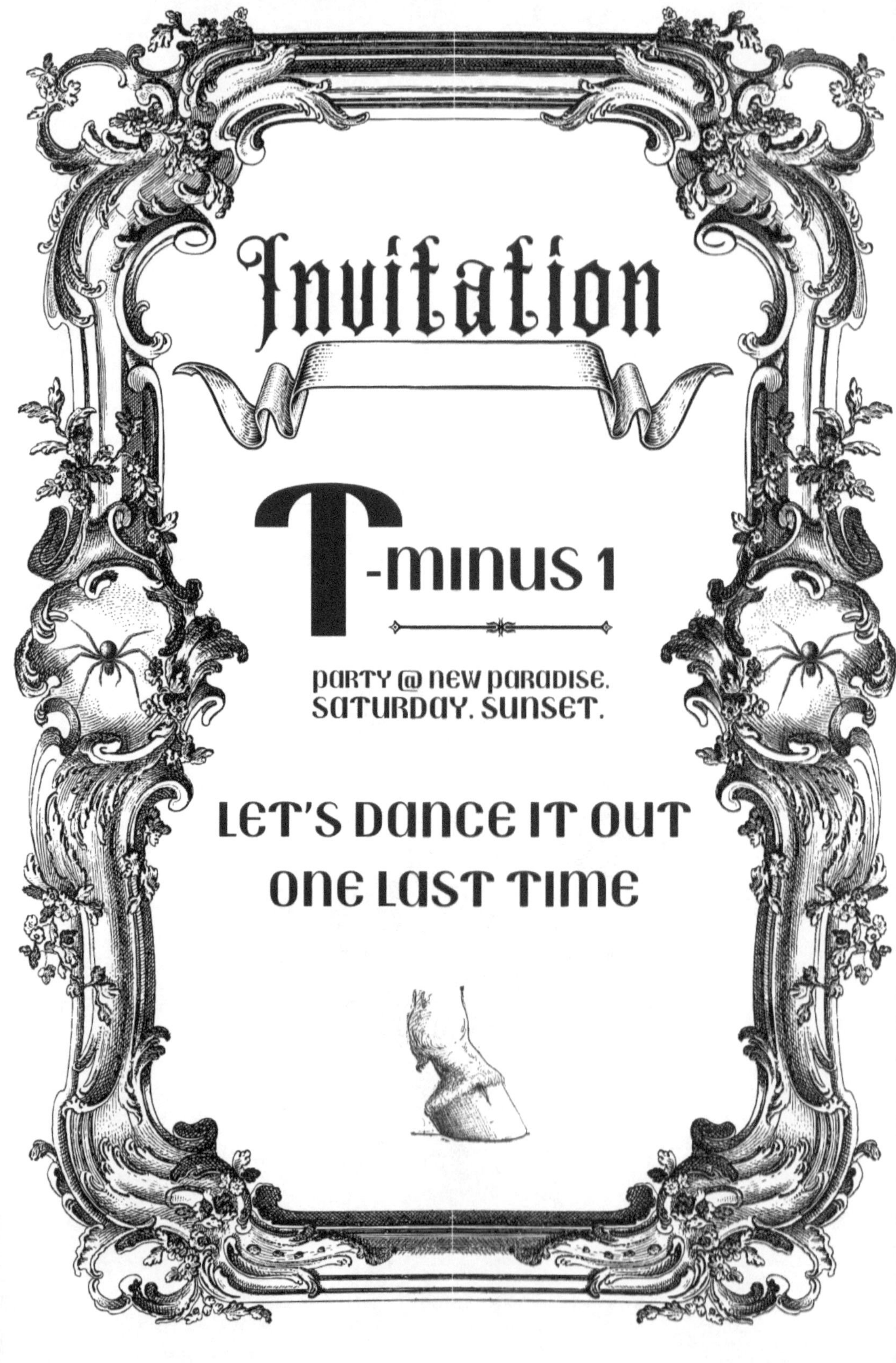
Invitation
T-minus 1
party @ new paradise.
saturday. sunset.
LET'S DANCE IT OUT
ONE LAST TIME

Cass, Angel of the Morning …

Thank you for your letter. And the ency-clopedia. How did you even find it? Here Collective's collection is a mess! I liked reading the entry you highlighted on Smilodon …

Tonight I took the long way around the neighborhood. Yes, at night!

I had to see the ship … Your ship.

I guess this is no place to be with a busted leg. I guess they need you up there to make the roads wide & light up the dark. I guess they need you more than I do.

Night felt so new today, I almost wrote a poem.

The vines give off a coolness. They've wrapped around some of our old ugly buildings, making them look like ancient ruins. Temples of forgotten gods: capitalism, civilization, law. On the Thare street overpass, you can see it, Galactic Exodus R.D.A. 3. (I always forget what the rest of that stands for — Romeo Deepspace Something?). It looks like a giant silver arcade … You're going to space in an arcade!

On Heare Street, I heard something behind me. A soft muffled thud. I was too afraid to turn around so I kept walking. I felt some-thing walk next to me. A presence. Against the busted brick wall that used to be a department store, I saw the shadow of a giant cat, ears perked up. I didn't turn & we walked on …

I'm not so arrogant as to say I've made a new friend but maybe we've come to an understanding.

I wish you were staying. I'm glad you're going. You're going to be a star! At least to me.

Tell me a story. What happened to Jay and Seb in the end? Happy ever after? Both of them staying here to be a mirror of each other for-ever? Wasn't there a story about a mirror that breaks into a thousand pieces and spreads across the earth, and it all works out in the end? Maybe that can be us, some day. All of us.

Yours in pieces,

Maxxy

~~The Snow Queen~~ *Server Farm Queen*

1. Search Engine

@creamland_techsupport
> Hello, thank you for visiting us at Creamland Ice Cream on Command. How can we please you today?

ID353626
> Hi. I'm one of your drivers, employee ID353626. I was on a delivery and my map started glitching. The truck is stalled.

@creamland_techsupport
> Hello, it's our pleasure to assist you. How can we please you today?

ID353626
> Hi. I can't see the next intersection, I guess I'm a few blocks past Heare St. The ice cream truck stalled. The self-driving mechanism went offline. The doors are on autolock. I need to know how to override the door mechanism so I can drive or get out.

@creamland_techsupport

> Hello, it's our pleasure to assist you. How can we help you today?

ID3536266

> I need help. Speak to agent. Manual override. Restart. RESTART.

@creamland_techsupport

> Hello, it's our pleasure to assist you, here is a menu of our current artisanal flavors. We have vanilla, chocolate, strawberry, straw poll, straw man argument, straw hats, strawng, indicating great prowess or physical power, strong love - lyrics to, strong man, man in the mirror, mirror mirror on the wall, mirror breaking, shards …

ID353626

> STOP. HELP. AGENT. COME ON. COME ON. Please.

@creamland_techsupport

> Shards, glass, walking on walking on broken glass, what you need to know about how to clean up broken glass shatter to drop or disperse to be everywhere glass shatter …

II. Grrrda in the Snow Storm

/ Sleep
Inbox: Refresh
Receipt Notification: **New message**

To: Grrrda
Subject: So how's the boy working out?

Message: [Empty white box. No message]

From:
> From the person who once asked
> never to hear from you again.

From: Robber Girl

Sent to you. Not to you in a list of many others, such as for an online fundraiser for this person or that, health or housing, relocation or surgery, and the *please help,* and you giving what you can, scrolling through the list to see who else is still around. Sent just to *you.*

From: Robber Girl to Grrrda.
Send time: 2am

The very witching time of night, when exes rise and remember your name.
On the computer screen, snow. A window to a snow storm. A search bar that has lost its ability to find. And this message.

Reply? N.
Reply? N.
Reply?

Replying is a very bad idea.

But you still reply.

From: Grrrda
To: Robber Girl
Subject: Re: So how's the boy working out?
Message:

~~What's it to you?~~
~~I thought we weren't talking.~~
Why are you asking?
Send.

Inbox: Refresh
Message: Save The Bees
Inbox: Refresh
Message: Keep your data safe!
Inbox: Refresh
Message: Air Purifiers Ship Free

No new messages.

Room = Empty white box: Twin mattress on floor; books, also on floor, spines bent; door to hallway closed but not locked; roommates gone; window, taped up with old sheets, four layers of duct tape. Don't look outside.

Behind the window, for the 229th day, snow. A new kind of storm now that snow is gone, a storm of information. Behind the cloth, the snow makes patterns on the glass, sometimes like letters, sometimes like the face of someone you really need to see, sometimes like hand prints, knocking, knocking.

A blizzard should be random. This one has algorithm, search results, information: *Crystalline ballet dancers, a chart mapping violent crime in a flood-prone city to consumption of ice cream, and then each individual ice cream flavor, and then a documentary about waffle cones, replays of a show where a group of friends work in an ice cream store, personality quiz.*

Stop.

Resist the temptation to remove the cloth and look out. Add tape. Calendar.

Add a |
There. Done.

For 229 days, the snow hasn't let up. Then again, neither have you. Survival. Survival of the *fittest. Fitness for survivors. Fitness first. Fitness centers near me. Turn on location services.* **Stop. Focus.**

Put on glasses. *Coke bottles. Polar Bears. Banksy. Warhol. Work of art. Do not be afraid of the - Meditation for a healthier - You could be at risk for - Symptoms include brain fog, losing sleep, sleeping too much, mood swings,* **Stop.**

The snow scrambles your brain. Better to look away. Keep information minimal. Keep thoughts simple. Avoid tangents.
Chair.
Table.
Bed.
Hardwood floor. Fake hardwood floor made of recycled plastic. *Plastic is information. Plastic carries messages. Seabirds choking. Turtles. Bags in the wind. Paper or paperorpaperor —*

REFRESH. CLEAR MIND. FOCUS.

"How's the boy?" Robber Girl asked you. The very *nerve* of that question. The boy did not work out, actually, not that it's any of her business. The boy opened a window and crawled out, leaving snowflakes on the floor. Snowflakes in the shape of an arrow, pointing straight into the endless white. *White Christmas All I want for Christmas is Last Christmas, I gave you my —*

"Did not work out" is one way to put it. You could also say he was not worth following a second time. The first time he left, back when you were both so young, you went after him. He was never really the same, except where he should have been different. This time, maybe you're different. Or maybe the snow is worse. You're not going to cry over him twice in some other bitch's ice palace, that's for sure.

Control N. *Open new window*. Static.
Search Bar: Anyone? No results.

Inbox: Refresh
Static.

Another snow day.
Turn away from the monitor. Heat soup in empty kitchen.
Ding. Notification.

Inbox (1)
From: Robber Girl
To: Grrrda
Subject: So how's the boy working out?
Re Previous message >> Why are you asking?

Don't be so excited.

Robber Girl to Grrrda, **Reply**: I need your help.

Open screen. New tab. Two tabs open is dangerous, a different way of communicating creates a new channel, duplicates *message duplicates information creates new pathways, more snow.* Your fingers are already typing.

You, typing:

Grrrda: Are you ok?
  Delete.
Grrrda: Do you know if anyone else still — ok?
  Delete.
Grrrda: I can't fucking believe you're texting me.

         Send.

    (…)

Immediate ellipses.
Meaning Robber Girl already had the chat tab open, so dangerous.
How long has she been waiting for your reply, exposed to the elements, exposed to snow?

Robber Girl: I know, but listen.
    (…)
Grrrda: You know radio frequencies are —
    (…)
Robber Girl: You're still so literal. Let me type.
    (…)
Grrrda: OK. fine. Type.
    (…)
Robber Girl: I need you to go out with me.
    (…)(pause, no typing)(…)
Grrrda: Out?
Robber Girl: Outside.
    (…)(pause, no typing)(…)
Grrrda: You're fucking with me. Out*side*?
    (……)
Robber Girl: It's important. I'm going. Tomorrow.
    Please? [Picture of round face smiling].

Look away. Emojis are images. *Images are fluid in meaning, invite multiple interpretations, create new pathways, more snow. Like people you love when they speak to you, create multiple meanings, pathways, mazes, labyrinths, superhighways, webs.*

Robber Girl: Tomorrow? Outside?

Close computer hard. Count to ten. Name three things that are solid: bones, wood, the window frame. Do not look outside. Do not even think about outside. Count colors you can identify: beige, taupe, gray, *gray matter, Grey's Anatomy, watch now? Grey Gardens. Gray hairs, this simple trick.* **Stop.**

Sleep is safe, go to sleep. You are not going out tomorrow. You could never find one another. Why would you risk this storm for Robber Girl when all you share is history?

What is history anyway?

> *History is*
> *History is a weapon*
> *History is written by the victors*
> *History is silent*
> *History repeats itself*
> *History is your browser history*
> *History is the last picture you took.*
> *Why did you take it?*
> *Name three things in that picture that*
> *no longer exist.*

III. Restore Browser History

Sleep does not tangent. Sleep has no sponsored algorithm. In sleep, you dream of the grandmas, the rose garden, the boy.

Once upon a time, before the snow, there were two houses, almost completely alike. They stood on either side of a street with a rose garden forming a skybridge between them.

The sky was any color you agreed on that week, but you remember it like this: a blue sky, pink rose bushes between two windows, and on a pink rosebud, a bee. Below, wide grassy side-walks, an electromagnetic tram, solar panels in every tree, bluebirds. Yes, of course, it was Augmented, programmed, not quite real. But it was real in the way that things we build together are always real.

Later, much later, when you met Robber Girl, you learned she did not grow up with Augments. She wanted to know everything. *Tell me about the texture of a thorn, the sound of a bee. You don't know how lucky you are.* Is it lucky to remember a bee? What does a bee look like? Resist the urge to open a browser tab. A bee looks like information looks like pixels. Yellow dot on a dot matrix of pink rose dots.

In these houses lived the Grandmas, Grandma One and Grandma Zero, legendary programmers who had built the houses line by line and rented them out to broke students like yourself. The grandmas never changed. They looked like their photos in the textbooks: Grandma One was Egyptian, short gray hair, cheek laceration from a rubber bullet in Tahrir Square. Grandma Zero was from Crown Heights and had refused to become a rabbi like her father. "Then you are not my son," he said, and she proved him right. The grandmas met at a sit-in at That Famous Tech School. They built our open-source Augment world. Retired, they sat in their programmed gardens and talked about their favorite neighborhood murders.

"She poisoned him, I tell you. She used rat poison. She must have put it into his breakfast cake. That's why he died so young."

"*Allahallah, how can you say that about our neighbor?*"

There was a broad pause as they both sipped their tea.

"… when we both know she snuffed him with a pillow."

And they both cackled, and then they kissed, and then they went into one or the other houses to enjoy their old love in the afternoon, flower petals falling down onto the cobblestones below. This is where you first met the boy. You were living in one grandma's house. He was living in the other. You first saw him covered in rose petals from the grandmas, pink petals in his long black hair, a broad smile.

Tell me again about the house, Robber Girl would say in the dark.

It wasn't all that, you said, searching for her hand.

Grandma One had everything all in gold. Gold bowls, water vase, brocade, gold numbers on every rented room including #3 where you lived. Grandma Zero had everything red, candles, books, doors, a red bed, where the boy slept. The houses were otherwise so similar you could forget which one was yours. Both were home.

When you told this story to Robber Girl, she asked, *why didn't you stay there forever?* She said, *it sounds stuffy. I would have left.* You asked her about growing up without Augments:

> \- carving into dry soil, softening
> concrete with an old mattress,
> wiring her first headset from an old
> motorcycle helmet. Drawing a door
> out of thin air and walking through.

Her answers made her even more special to you and for a time they filled you with shame, then for a while, you blamed her, and anti-augmenters like her, for the snow. Because the snow eventually came, one disordered snowflake at a time, shifting things that should have been random into new frightening weather patterns, server overload climate change.

It wasn't too bad at first: one afternoon instead of a flower pot, there was a basket of snakes. Instead of a teapot, there was a tiny pond icing over for winter. Instead of an armchair, there was a park bench. We put up with the bench for a long time, even though it was cold and hard.

"There's something wrong with my lenses," you and the boy said. The snow was almost funny: Grandma One's hair going pink, water flowing up into the faucet, instead of down.

Then one day, it wasn't funny: there were words about tooth-paste on the kitchen counter; there were two of everything. One day, any cupboard you opened contained loud angry voices demanding help, or access, or the end of it all.

The grandmas stayed up late talking. You knew it was serious when they stopped laughing. One morning they took off their glasses. We took off our lenses. There was still a world underneath. It wasn't a wasteland like in some science fiction movie. It was just bland. Beige. Boring. Undecorated. Like ours is now, minus the snow. We put our lenses back on.

Then the snow began to fall both inside and outside our glasses.

Everyone knows that the grandmas were the first to leave. When the snow covered the ground, they packed up backpacks and walked away together, leaving their glasses on the red kitchen counter. The rosebuds faded. Sometime later, the boy went too. "I'm going to control the snow," he said, and you followed him.

❧

The last time you saw the grandmas, you were looking for the boy. You were trekking through the snow with Robber Girl, hand in hand, when you stumbled into their huts made of animal skins, old cars, and whatever else they could find.

They let you stay three days, then they made you both leave.

"Too corruptible," Grandma Zero said.

"Cruft," said Grandma One.

They were right. You could not see one thing without wanting another.

When you found the boy, he was living in a new program: an ice castle city, with others paving layers of snow on snow. You thought you could make it work together, you, the boy, and Robber Girl. When she gave you a choice, you chose the boy, if only because you resented having to make a choice.

It is believed that the grandmas are still out there, that they've learned to build their own village, a place with real rosebuds, and real bricks heated in the fire, a stream of water quicksilvered with salmon, the hum of real bees. The only catch is: how do you find it, how can you survive long enough to get there, what if it doesn't exist?

IV. Search Engine

/Sleep.

Open new tab. Close tabs quickly. Open Map. Zoom out. Snow.

Stare at white.

Set pin. Zoom out. More snow.

Pop Up: Order self driving car?

Pop-up, you *lie*. There are no more self-driving cars.

The last word on this is that you can order a car but it won't arrive. If it arrives, and you get in, it will strand you somewhere out there in the snow, iterating destinations. There are several people in the chatrooms locked in cars. Their comments go from bemused "guys guys, guess what" to despair to infrequent. Their messages turn snowy.

What is a map when information creates its own geography?

Are there bees out there?

Look at the window. You could lift the cover. Look for bees. Buzzing. *Vibration. Notification. Pollination. Share. Like. Like. Like.*

Breathe. Refresh. Clear mind. Do not look out.

❧

The boy and you, that was not meant to last. He wanted more: freedom, disruption, innovation. He walked across a blue-lit stage with a headset and people got to their feet. He made buildings, whole neighborhoods, just to house information. "More power," he said. His body was cold at night.

What did the boy have? Big ideas, lustrous hair, a trail from belly button to — well, who cares now? *A happy trail. A road to perdition. A single lane highway. A one track* — **Stop.**

What did Robber Girl have? Robber Girl was quote unquote real. Her words. She had stubbornness, courage to hop data trains, sleep under the stars. Robber Girl had convictions that were impossibly complicated, *just unplug*. She had survival skills: a knife,

187

fur, pelts, warmth, a way of keeping things close and immediate when you needed it most. Robber Girl had stupid ideas like, "Let's just walk out into the snow." And now wants you to go with her.

Open new window. Feel the sweep of cold fear.

Grrrda: Why do you want to go into the snow?

Robber Girl: I can't tell you yet.

Trustworthy? Y/N.

Yes: Robber Girl has never lied, let anyone down; she called it like it was at every moment, even that one time when you made it so hard to tell the truth.

Open Browser History

"If I stay with the boy, will you leave?"

"Yes."

Close Browser History

No: Robber Girl Gets out of control.

Open Chat Window

Grrrda: You held a knife to my throat.

Robber Girl: You wanted me to.

Grrrda: Not all the time, you asshole. Some days, I just wanted —

[Bees]

[Peace]

[Soup]

[Something other than *fight*]

404 Not Found

> Grrrda: Why do you think I can
> help you?

Pause. Silence. And then.

Because you're good in a crisis.
  Because you're incorruptible.
    Because you survived. We survived.
      Because you're the only one who can keep me steady.
        Because there's no one else left.

Close windows. The duct tape on the outside window threatens to unpeel at any moment. Then it hits you: Robber Girl knows where the grandmothers are. She must. Otherwise why go?

How to survive the information blizzard: Count. Breathe. Clear mind. Do not seek out more information.

Then again, it's no life here, focusing on Chair. Table. Bed. Waiting for the end of a storm that has no end.

Open browser window:

> Grrrda: Ok.
> Robber Girl: Ok?
> Grrrda. Ok. I'll go with you into the snow.
> Robber Girl: [Smiley Face Emoji]
> Grrrda: Stop that! There's literally no one else left?
> Robber Girl: No one better than you.

Just like that, you get to feel furious and wanted all at the same time.

You look around your room for perhaps the last time. Add a

|.

Bed. Table. Chair.

Shove them aside.

Peel the corner of the duct tape on the right hand side of the window.

V. Open A New Window

As for there being almost no one else left:

The snow storm is iterative. Those who let the snow in become scattered. Their words become nonsense. Filler. Ads. Memes. And then silence. Avalanche. Flood. We don't know why some people resist and why most wander into the snow.

We know what not to do:

Do not iterate. Do not click on things. Do not open multiple tabs. Limit contact. Close windows.

Avoid looking outside, getting sucked into the vastness of information and uncertainty and body shame and want and things to buy and read and like.

Maybe you survived the great blizzard outside because you'd already been through a cataclysm: when Robber Girl left you, she stood with her back to the only door and gave you *her* storm, an avalanche of information beginning every line with *you*, and ending with cold. Avalanche: an unstable mass breaks off from the bank, picking up speed as it moves downhill, producing a suffocating river of snow.

You barely survived.

> [[Focus on the counter. Name
> three things: Toothbrush. Crack all
> the way down the middle of the
> wall. Ribcage as ruined house that
> lets in snow. Make a list of people
> to whom you can say "I love you."]]

Now put on long pants, long sleeves. You would tell your roommates you're going out, but there is no one left to tell.

You don't need to ask Robber Girl where to meet. Two terrible men, a racist professor Heare and a misogynist writer Thare left streets named after them and created an intersection. It was always agreed between you that in case of emergency, you would find one another between Heare and Thare.

You peel off the last tape. The protective sheet falls to the ground.

⁂

The snow hits the window: shape of a rose. Shape of a B, for lack of remembering actual bees. Shape of the quadratic equation from Algebra 101. Shape of your first childhood dog, who died, thanks very much for the reminder.

You take the chair. You hoist it over your head. You throw it at the window.

The window does not shatter. It just rearranges: shard, opening, snow.

⁂

Chatroom. A few months ago. People theorizing:

"The algorithms didn't break. They adapted."

"That's stupid. Algorithms aren't alive."

"If they're not alive, then why are they evolving?"

Outside, the snow takes the shape of a pair of shoes you almost bought. Here they are rendered in static-white, fuzzing along the sides. The snow invites you to reach out to a friend who has been dead for four years. The snow points in the direction of everything all at once and also a single frog that mewls like a kitten.

The key to navigating the blizzard is to focus as much as possible on what you are looking for. To remember what it feels like to walk. Now your bare feet are on the frozen ground, every single step dull and painful. You walk down a narrow street under a highway filled with stalled self-driving cars, and everywhere, on the roof of the cars, piled into drifts, on the dark lampposts, snow.

Where it falls, the snow makes scenes: three people dancing by the ocean, gone; birthday cake, gone; boxes full of toys, a bear tumbling out, gone.

There are also real objects left behind: coke bottles, wrappers, rubber tubing for IVs, a wig, beads, letters in a jumble. Twelve monkeys could take this and make up the world again, given forever. *Forever stamps. Forever new. Forever credit card. Return policy.*

Focus. Think of a memory.

⁂

When you met Robber Girl, you found her in a clearing tending to a tiny plant in the sun. Her thick legs in small shorts, one foot on a box, not a care in the world. A crop top, a belly, bulging arms and even bigger muscles. The plant was a whisper of a green thing. When you waved your hand over it trying to right-click for information, nothing happened. It was real. She laughed.

Now, between Heare and Thare is a figure with strong arms. Static. You approach. The figure backs up. You back up. They come closer. You know algorithms don't have personalities, but if they did, you'd curse them for making such an obviously petty program.

You close your eyes, and invite the past.

Past: Robber Girl, tending to a small plant. Her laugh. The soft green leaves.

Present: You feel her approaching. You wonder what she is imagining of you, what memories you left her, of the kind that make one smile. Table. Bed. Chair.

You call up another memory, you and Robber Girl laughing under blankets that smelled like rain and body oil.

You feel her close.

You reach across, remembering the feel of her hand, picturing a tiny tendril, soft leaves.

And predictably, #onbrand, when you and Robber Girl finally touch, it's not a meeting of fingertips like a chapel ceiling. You slam into one another hard, feel their hard-ass head against your jaw and instinctively grab their soft-ass belly to pull them away, and how you loved that belly, but it's gone from your hands and then you're staring at one another in the snow, and it's Robber Girl and Grrrda, reunited for one last show.

You look down first.

Search Bar. When you look at an image (eg. a former love-of-your-life), what are you looking at?

    (a) Inverted rod and cone party on the back of a retina;
    (b) Projection onto cave wall;
    (c) Pixels gathered;
    (d) Memory, comparison;
    (e) Nothing, anymore, it being all snow.

The snow whirls around, but you ignore it because here is something you can focus on.

Effects of age and distance and change on the person you loved:
    1) Facial hair where there was smoothness before;
    2) Gray hair cut short;

3) Receding hairline, strengthening jaw;
4) Wrinkles, laugh and frown lines you didn't help make,
that were not there before;

Open a chat box, mid-air.
"New name?" you ask, too casually.
"RG."
"Nice to re-meet you, RG. What the fuck are we doing here?"

Time evolves information, like skin: lines, patterns, tracks. These changes that happened without you, they hurt. The worst part of the snow is the constant reminder that stories no longer need us. You sign in weeks later and there's a whole thing about a toaster and a crocodile that everyone has already laughed at before you could begin to understand.

RG grabs your hand. The pressure on your skin is information. RG and Grrrda. You + RG. You re-enter, not too reluctantly, into that *we*.

We, you and RG, hold hands and walk through the snow, and even though you hate RG with all the love you have, your body remembers them. The snow makes shapes around you: the shape of a duck and a crocodile being friends. You walk on, "Winter Wonderland" playing on loop in your brain: *in the meadow we can build a — in the meadow we can build a — in the meadow we can build.*

VI. Who Drives the Ice Cream Truck in The Snowpocalypse?

> Grrrda to RG: So you know where
> the grandmas are?

RG looks back at you, smiles mysteriously, confusingly.

We are avatars in the information desolation wilderness. Snowflakes are dangling like comment threads, iterating and iterating and iterating, and referring back to one another, falling and rising again, reiterating. We hold hands. You punch RG in the shoulder hard to help them focus and they punch back, except RG knows exactly where to find the pressure point at the deltoid attachment with one knuckle, and it hurts like hell, but for a minute you can see, and there is a shape ahead that looks like not-snow.

"There it is," RG says.

"The grandmas?"

RG's response is muffled.

You walk on, shivering.

In the storm, the shape delineates itself: a big hulking thing, bigger than us. We walk towards it. You carefully, RG determinedly. Before you have time to repeat, "Is that the grandma village?" you realize it is not.

It is: an ice cream truck, overturned. One of the ice cream trucks that was all the rage when the snow kept everyone home. Pink, white, polka dots, app-interfaced to deliver ice cream within 15 minutes anywhere in town. Like so many other cars, it got stuck out here.

There is a moment when you think RG brought you out for ice cream. That you wandered into the blizzard in search of the last pint of mint chocolate. You almost laugh.

RG drops your hand and rushes to the ice cream truck. There is a strange bulge in the side, as if someone had tried to kick their way out.

RG puts a hand on the window.

Hand on window = Message.

On the other side of the window, despite the snow, movement. A hand slowly comes to the window, fitting into the print.

Hand on other side of window = Message received.

Chat window:

Grrrda to RG: Who is this now?

You understand quickly. We are not here on a date. We are here for this person in the ice cream truck. Your lungs ice with disappointment, but you start moving because RG was right. You are the best person to help. You know how to program, debug, repair. This does not mean you know how to love.

"Let's get them out," you say.

Snow in the shape of a question mark, interrobang, wtf.

By the side of the road, a selfie stick, a wig, a set of AR glasses, one lens broken. You retrieve the stick, wedge it under the door. You take turns, you and RG, fighting the door.

"You lied to me."

"I didn't lie," RG says, tapping on the window. The person on the other side taps back.

"You said we were going to the grandmas."

"I never said that. You said that."

"You said you needed my help." You hit the wedged stick hard with your fist. The automatic doors resist.

"I do."

Your hands have gotten soft.

Mood: I want to go home. Chair, table, bed.

The snow around you shows you shapes:

Shape of you and RG in bed, their shoulder blades shaped like a mountain. Shape of your hurt that RG is here because after all that they found a love worth chasing into the storm.

You can't tell who you are jealous of, but some petty thing in you is rising like a whale from a nature documentary, and it surfaces now.

You shove RG aside. You thump on the window and yell *back up*, and you thrust the stick so hard at the glass that it cracks, a proper break, and your shoulder hurts, and you wrench RG's jacket off and use it to wrap your hand and punch out the shards.

"Come the fuck out then," your words already disappearing in the snow.

⋙

Flashback, Restore Browser History.

The grandmas. The boy. The Augmented Garden, far, far back in time, before the snow.

A memory of Grandma One in her gold glasses, staring off into the distance, the index finger of her left hand twitching, looking like an old woman with tremors, but you knew she was coding, building, repairing: a white marble stairway spiraled upward leading up through a marble arch, and down to the blue sea, a jungle with yellow butterflies. She paused to speak to you.

"Dear, the program is not about making things up." She waved an arm through the air like a wand. Gold filaments flew across a marble ballroom three times the size of the entire house, gold brocade walls, a gold floor.

"It's about making things better," the boy said, inspecting the mirrored walls, looking for a seam.

Grandma Zero gently pulled the boy's hand away from the wall, and then not so gently twirled him into waltz position. "It's about remembering," and snapped her fingers to make an invisible orchestra play.

You bowed to Grandma One. She laughed and stepped into the dance with you. And in that dance, you learned to program. You remembered, from a book, the idea of lily pads. You asked the chandelier to separate itself into dozens of lanterns, set them free to float on the mirrored ceiling. You invited blue velvet to unfurl from all four corners like an ocean. And you all laughed.

The person who comes out of the truck looks like she's been stuck in there for a long time. Her cheeks are sallow. Her braids are grown out. Her legs wobble. But when you look at the way RG looks at her, your heart breaks because together they are *perfect*.

Ice Cream's first words, through chapped lips: "What can I get for you?"

RG's first words, through tears of relief: "Are you out of pistachio?"

They laugh and hug again.

RG introduces you. "This is Grrrda. a friend."

Not even *their* friend. A friend. Somebody's friend. Surely, in this snow storm, there is someone to whom you are friend.

Ice Cream hugs you too. Her hug is strong for someone stuck in an ice cream truck for days.

Now she leans against the truck, crying relief, with RG petting her gently. And she is absolutely a person worth risking a snow storm to go find.

"I'll just — I'll —" you say, and walk off to give them space. You feel their love behind you, like a sunset at your back, and then like an explosion.

You think: Maybe I can find the grandmas.

Go into the woods and meet your grandma, take her this cake and this pot of butter, stay on the path.

RG: Let's go back.
Grrrda: Ok.

VII. Abyss, Staring Back

Walk forward. Do not turn back. If you turn back, you will see the both of them, the way their bodies fit together, and how they walk.

Is there anything sweeter than two people in a snowstorm holding hands?

By the side of the road, a box of cell phones, some of them ringing. By the side of the road, a river, two boots. One boot fits. You have one cold foot.

They laugh behind you, and for a minute you laugh too. The snow clears.

Memories intrude.

One. The Boy in the Ice Palace, his frustration. How he would sit up at night, trying to fit the pieces of the puzzle together, and finally froze, his face a blue screen. How you watched over his shoulder until you thought of sleeping outdoors with RG, how stars fit together in the sky, and you solved the puzzle and freed him. He didn't talk to you for three days.

Two. The time you made RG a program: a beach with working waves, flying fish you'd copy-pasted from archives, a bar you could swim up to and sit on smooth rocks and a sunset. RG had said, *sorry, this is just — not my thing.*

Three. The time after RG left when you ran into them at a party and hushed the entire crowd by opening a source window and deprogramming RG's body from the space, rendering them invisible for fifteen minutes. How you blamed the snow, but at least two people saw you go:

```
<open>
spite command:
/robbergirl
<close>
```

You wonder how much of that RG remembers now. You look back. RG catches your eye. One thick eyebrow comes up, *don't start.* Of course they remember everything. If the grandmas never find us before it's too late, if every library fritters into snow, tell them we contain all the knowledge within us. We don't need the greatest minds of our generation to discover the black hole information paradox. No information is ever lost. Ask your ex.

"So how do you two know each other?" — Ice Cream Person.

400 BAD REQUEST.

"We go way back." RG.

"We go way back" = "we are never fucking again."

There is something on the horizon. Lines. Iteration. Search. Nothing found.

Keep looking.

RG and Notyou, whose name is Ays, which sounds like "ice" and is the queer-half-name for Aysha, hold hands. You follow, like the street cleaner at the end of a parade.

On the third day, or maybe just the third hour, RG and Ays stop suddenly. A giant hole opens in front of you, in the ground. The snow-covered path opens into an empty space that you feel deep in your chest.

> Delete
> Delete

No effect.

Here is a bridge, hanging over a dark expanse. Across the bridge, the path goes homeward. And below the bridge, there is something worse than snow.

Class Program: {Static Void}.

You remember this code.

An end to the snow. And nothing else but a quivering kind of emptiness. To the left and right of you, snow. And beyond the bridge, home.

And beyond the snow?

The possibility of the code equivalent of smelling fish soup and warmth.

The bridge that carries over the {Static Void} has one entry point, and is only two lines deep.

```
eval(footstepInput) //
Class Program {static void main
>2 = voidall}
```

You read the code so easily, it feels strange RG and Ays can't. This code is not meant for three. It's meant for two.

You call a sidebar with RG.

```
Grrrda: We are not going to make
it across.
RG: We can at least try. You
never know when to try.
Grrrda: You never know when to
stop trying.
<end transmission>
```

Around us, snow in the shape of a basketball and a body falling upwards towards it, ball round and spine arced like the moon and sun.

```
<open transmission>
Grrrda: You always think things
are better than they are;
RG: You always make everything
worse.
Grrrda: You never gave me a
chance.
```
Ays Has Joined The Chat
```
Ays: Hey, just thought you
should know the snow is getting
worse.
```

She's right, the snow is getting worse, battering the thin ropes of code across the void. You try to picture you, and RG, and Ays making it over the bridge together, coming home. The thing is, you can't.

> Grrrda: You and Ays go. I'll find another way.
> RG: What other way?
> Grrrda: I'm going into the snow.
> *Ays, RG — Typing.*
> RG: You won't make it.
> Grrrda: I'm going to find the grandmothers.
> *Grrrda has ended the chat.*

They stare at you, question marks crystallizing above them. You wave them on.

Open Browser History:

    a)   What RG has taught you: to be brave, to jump head first.

    b)   What the boy has taught you: to trust your memory.

The boy was not entirely wrong. You can't control information, but you can:

> :Find a point that doesn't change
> >Breathe.
> >Think of fishbone soup and stories. Think of gossip.
> Clear cache. Refresh. Find source code.
> Open Door: (
> Allow in one.
> Enter.

You walk alone into the snow.

> Close door
>)
> Let information in. Become everything.

VIII. Mirrors

One day, someone will want to know how the snow storm came about. Let's just say that there was once a magic mirror, and we kept it going with love, and hope, and our capacity to care about one another. For a time, despite every evil intention, it succeeded in bringing us some morsels of joy. Then the mirror broke. And now, here we are, clinging to what little is solid: *chair, table, bench, pasta, try this simple trick* — stop.

The first thing you feel when you walk into the snow is the absence of feeling. *So you disappeared, how would you know?* Maybe you can't see your hands in front of your face. You raise your hands. They are now cat paws. *Sure, you think, why not.* Now they are actual cats, calico, and tabby, and black, and white, sitting at a piano. You laugh, because the theory about all information being cats was right all along, and when you laugh, you laugh cats, and when you breathe in to laugh again, you breathe in fur, lungs gasping for air, drowning, throat raw.

The cats disappear. In front of you now, fragile and shiny as if through cellophane, is a world you never got to see: a sunset over a pond, cattails; manta rays cutting the ocean, a fennec fox disappearing between two sand dunes. Then there are two foxes — a reflection, and a real one — and a place between, where the mirror has let you in. It feels like a cold blast pulling at your skin, your logins, your credentials. Your name is the first thing to go, and then hair. Now when you look at the snow, you see no images, only code, glittering like diamond dust.

Along the way of becoming Snow, you find your programming, and where it has failed.

Programming:
{Must Rescue Boy.

{If there is no boy, assume there is no one to rescue.
Standby, wait for boy.
{If there are many boys, assume first of sequence.
/ END program.

{Body hierarchy:
    {not yours
    /END Program.

{Information distraction from seeing ourselves,
moments.
      /END SLEEP.

And then everything goes white, goes information, goes cats, goes stars.

IX. Tea With Muhammed

Status Update: Final.

Imagine a self picture.

Grrrda, me, released from the snow. In a desert.

"Like," says a voice.

I open my eyes.

The snow is gone. The ground is — well, it's ground. Un-augmented. Some concrete. Many weeds. And sand.

A woman is standing before me, the sun behind her. She wears no augment glasses. She is ageless. She takes *my* {non cat, non flesh hand}. I struggle to identify her without a search bar. Maybe one of the grandmas, an old one from the stories: Katherine Johnson; Ada Lovelace. Hypatia. She pulls me to my feet. We walk over the sand towards a village with low sand-colored houses and bright green palm fronds. She says, in a voice of many, "come meet my friend."

We stop at a desert house with tall windows and grooves to catch the wind. A red tapestry hangs over the vaulted doorway.

Search Bar: Where are we?

"Clue One," says the maybe-grandma. "Iran, home of a mathematician."

"Clue Two." He wanted to be known by his region, *al-kharizmi*. From Kharizmi. AlKharizmi became Al-Ghorithmi, and then algorithm.

Inside, a man sits at a table, leaning over scrolls. I can tell he is completing a program because of the way the air shimmers around him, this person for whom algorithm means home.

Above his scrolls, a circle forms, gold. It flies up. The circle hovers in the air and teaches the air to create two new circles. Each circle holds a moment in time, preserving the other in memory, a snapshot, information.

Muhammad Ibn Musa smiles, tucks a lock of hair back into his turban, beard glittering in the light.

A potential of infinite circles: an oasis not run over by sand or snow, a mirror showing only dunes, maybe beyond it, an ice cream truck, two bodies in one moment that is not augmentable.

Muhammad Ibn Musa Al Kharizmi, original grandma, takes a break from completing the circle to boil water over the fire. Tea leaves spin.

I cannot wake myself from this dream within a dream. A story or a code can't write itself into being. Or can it? I watch the ice cream truck leave the circle. They are off to create moments that are not programmed. Maybe there is some other adventure for me. I turn to Muhammad for a moment which is not replicable, and which is therefore perfect. He hands me a cup.

Table, teacup, dates, cushion, floor. Hands.

Floor. Cushion. Table. Dates. Teapot. Cup. Hands. Warmth. Steam rising from a cup. Silence.

Dear Seb, The One Who Remembers,

I took the liberty of putting this book in your backpack.

I came to New Paradise to kiss you one last time. I thought, *a kiss in the headlights of a spaceship.* How you would have loved the drama. How I might have loved my revenge.

I stood outside New Paradise a long time, listening as the light and music spilled out, watching bodies move through the tiny space with so many of us crammed inside. I hate a third of these people. I love (and have loved) a third of them. I only know the others from brief moments: hauling rocks, arguing about actions, tossing sandbags, a smile, a kiss, a dance.

I told myself I wasn't looking for you, but I was. As my eyes adjusted, I thought, "Take a last look. You won't see them again." And that's how in looking for you, I found myself seeing like you. Remembering.

I know you're smiling as you read this. You know exactly what I mean.

I saw a short-haired queer with thick furring hands. They leaned against the wall outside, watching the sky as if thirsting for snow. I see others like them too: bird-types, bears, an ocelot I know who is indeed a lot. By the bar, Maxxy was dancing with Ali and with a tall queer with an anchor tattoo who smelled like the ocean. Maxxy kissed them both. I saw Cass learning to spin in the wheelchair B. Collective found, lights on the backrest like a throne, a lumberjack butch with spiky gray hair, a femme with a tattoo-map of where monarch butterflies used to roost, RG tending the vines that pour through the window framing a portrait of Paradise DeVine as we remember her, one hand on her hip ready to sing.

By the time I found you, I was covered in everyone's sweat, like a book passed down from hand to hand, changed just a little bit along the way.

And there you were: in the sleeveless shirt you cut so deep it's barely a shirt at all. Your strong, soft back, and your tattoo, just the word *And.* Your eyes were closed, like they always were when you danced. You didn't stop when you elbowed Ali in the ribs. He didn't care. He was smiling, his great work complete. B. Collective got us 100 tickets. We'll never know how.

I wanted to wake you from your dance, like I always wanted to wake you, with a kiss. I know exactly what you'd say. Look, you'd say, and tear up uselessly. This is our *once.*

But I didn't. Because the idea came to me, the idea I did not know had been shifting around in my head. At The old Paradise, after the fire, after the wave, the rubble, watching the vines that only grow after disaster reach for the stars, a new planet creating itself right here under our feet, a *what if* that hit me so hard, I laughed. A *what if* that said: *why does the only storyteller always have to be you?*

So here's your book back, Seb. There's a story inside for you to continue. It's going to need your stubborn, petty, perfect memory to tell it right. Or at least to turn whatever strange configurations of life you find into woods.

I like to think that one day we'll be here together again. No matter what has happened, how space and life have changed us, I think we'll see one another and know. You can always tell who's in your story. No distance of space or time has ever changed that.

See you in the after,

Jay

Galactic Exodus
G.E.R.D.A. 3
Admit Only One
GGW8wUxOZX
Bon Voyage
Remember Us

Gratitude

Welcome to the acknowledgments! I'm so glad you're here. Below are some of the most wonderful, joyful, brilliant people you could ever meet. I wouldn't be here without their kindness, inspiration, love, and generosity. May I introduce you?

I first want to thank Stelliform Press for the conversations you bring, the people you gather, and for having me. Astronomical thanks to Selena Middleton, captain, visionary, artist, advocate, magician. Where any reasonable editor and press might have said, let's simplify, Selena said what if, and invited in the wildest and best version of what this book could be — you make the world bigger and you made this book what it is. Thanks to Ren Hutchings for being part of that vision, and for being such a force of imagination and generosity in this world. Thanks also to Stelliform writers for being such a brilliant and kind and magnificent community. What an honor it is to be in this conversation with you.

Thank you to Carly AF (Carlydraws.com) for this cover that is beyond my wildest dreams. Thank you to Zeph Fishlyn (Zephrocious.com) for your illustrations in this book and your art in the world. Thank you to Selena Middleton, also mentioned above, for bending the limits of form and formatting. You brought Seb and Jay's world to life.

Thanks to Tora Brumalis for your being an incisive and caring sensitivity reader on *Playlist for Merx Love.*

Thanks to queer spaces and the people who keep them going, especially Hasta Muerte, El Rio, The Stud, The White Horse, and Grandma's Discount Dungeon. This book was written there and so was I.

A big thank you to the art spaces that have welcomed and supported me: The Mineral School (thank you Jane Hodges), Clarion West (thank you Neile Graham and Jae Steinbacher), OSU's Shotpouch Residency, Tin House, Lambda, Club Chicxulub (thank you Matt Carney, Lauren Johnson, my apocalyptically stylish friends), F(r)iction (thank you Helen Maimaris and Emily Brill-Holland, genius editors), the SF Olympians Festival (thanks to Stuart Bousel for Giant Bones, for taking a chance on my singing sailors, and for your friendship).

To everyone at Clarion West 2018. You have all been the stars in my sky. Your books, your stories, your words around that table, your ways of being in the world light my path. Special thanks to those of you I've gotten to speak with often while I was writing this book: Isabel Cañas, Ewen Ma, Ben Pladek, Natalia Theodoridou, Jen Sexton-Riley, and to E.C. Barrett, dearest friend, for Krakens, brilliant conversation, collaboration, reframes, laughter. There will never be enough thanks.

To my SFSU, Bay Area, and Lambda writing communities: Miah Jeffra (thank you for walks and lunches and joy), Julián Delgado Lopera, Luke Dani Blue, Jane McDermott; to Chad Koch, Philip Harris, Ploi Pirapokin, you know too much and I love you; to Michelle Carter, Nona Caspers, and Anne Galjour for your mentorship; to the friends who have accompanied me on this journey: Samuel Rigel Bowman, Liz Michaud, Rawiyah Tariq, Ammi Keller, Nara Dahlbacka, Whitney Porter, Lizzie Tran, Celeste Chan, Kathryn Kruse, Heidi Kasa, and the writers whose adventures I've gotten to be part of: Ilana Kramer, Charles Smith, Cailey Hall, Vivian Underhill, Mackenzie Studebaker, Rook Riley, Stacey Matthews-Winn, Jordan Godwin, Skyellen Kulanu, and Eming Piansay.

Special thanks to my batshit twin Raven, and separately to Marie Sinclair, I love you both so much; to Nancy Au, you've taught me so much about being a friend and artist in this world, and I love you; to Nicole Jost — our collaboration is one of the best things I've ever done. Our friendship is even better; to Jenna Leah and Lauren Sapala for dragging me out of various closets; to Summer Fletcher, my brother, for love and endless laughs, GFY. To Samar Hijazi and Carole Faroux, I carry your friendship with me always. To Carine Hejazi, for your bravery and shared joy. And to Anna L., wherever you are, for that afternoon at Machiavelli's house especially.

To my family I lucked my way into: April and Kenan (I love you mom and B Bro), and Marc, Jenny, Brian, Lawrence, and Ann, you are inspirations. To the aunties: Maria, Kari, Catrien, Karen, Laurie, Amy, Ayse, Lucienne — you are my original storytellers. And to the family I came to by falling in love: Haven (always and forever my Da Wao, and one of my favorite people forever, I love you and am so proud of you), Hilary Reed and Cedre Csillagi for so much joy and laughter and inspiration, and to the Daddies, Jeff and Chris. To Marge "Maj the Traveler" Carlson, and the Kuhne brothers, John and Scott, who have all the answers.

To the cats: Smaug (Rest in Greatness), Midnight, and Pain Perdu (on my shoulder as I write this) who are here to love the light and make tiny holes in my skin and furniture. Thank you.

To Kadet Beker/Beckett Kuhne, my wife, husbat, soulmate, and greatest collaborator. It was always the joy of this dance and conversation and adventure with you that makes it all worth it. I can't believe I found you. Ya'aburnee.

To those I will have inevitably forgotten on this list, you are here and you know it. I can't wait to dance with you again!

And if your eyes are on this, to you. Whether #TeamEarth or #TeamShip, thank you for being part of this voyage with me. And now the story belongs to you.

About the Author

Syr Hayati Beker is a nonbinary Turkish-French-USian writer, immersive experience creator, and horror nerd in search of the queer love language of climate change. They are a graduate of Clarion West, Lambda's Emerging Writers Fellowship, and have an MFA from SFSU. Syr is the co-founder of Queer Cat Productions performing arts company and The Escapery Collective. Their work appears in *Foglifter*, *Joyland*, *Fairy Tale Review*, *F(r)iction*, *Michigan Quarterly Review*, *Spunk*, *Gigantic Sequins*, *Home is Where you Queer Your Heart* (Foglifter Press, 2021), and in theaters, pirate ships, galleries, and queer bars near you. You can find them at SyrBeker.com, which is definitely not haunted.

Image Credits

Maxxy's drawing of the bathroom door at The Paradise is adapted from a photograph of graffiti of a quote from Murray Bookchin on a bathroom door at the University of Brest (Brittany, France, October 22, 2022).[1]

The photograph is listed under a Creative Commons "Share Alike" license. The photograph is used as a base, with the graffiti at the top and bottom of the original image preserved. In the spirit of this license and the original image, we invite human collaborators to modify and share the bathroom door image, with credit to Syr Hayati Beker and Stelliform Press. We reach out especially to other queer community spaces to use this image to imagine your future queer space conversations.

The "Full Color Illustrations" of Little Red Riding Hood,[2] The Little Matchgirl,[3] and The Little Mermaid[4] are all in the public domain. The illustrations are in the public

---

[1] "Graffiti d'une citation de Murray Bookchin." Photograph. Accessed July 18, 2025. Wikimedia Commons contributor Emgann444, "File:Graffiti d'une citation de Murray Bookchin.jpg," Wikimedia Commons, https://commons.wikimedia.org/w/index.php?title=File: Graffiti_d%27une_citation_de_Murray_Bookchin.jpg.

[2] Schmidhammer, Arpad. 1905. *Little Red Riding Hood*. Illustration. Accessed July 18, 2025. Wikimedia Commons contributors, "File: Arpad Schmidhammer- Červená karkulka (1905).jpg," Wikimedia Commons, https://commons.wikimedia.org/w/index.php?title= File:Arpad_Schmidhammer-_%C4%8Cerven%C3%A1_karkulka_ (1905).jpg.

domain in the United States because they were published (or registered with the U.S. Copyright Office) before January 1, 1905, 1921 and 1930 respectively.

[3] Hardy, E. Stuart. 1921. *The Little Match Seller*. Illustration. Accessed July 21, 2025. https://www.childstories.org/en/the-little-match-seller-1921.html.

[4] Dulac, Edmund. 1930. *The Little Mermaid*. Illustration. Accessed July 18, 2025. Wikimedia Commons contributors, "File:Little Mermaid - mermaids treasures - Edmund Dulac for Andersen.jpg," Wikimedia Commons, https://commons.wikimedia.org/w/index.php?title=File:Little_Mermaid_-_mermaids_treasures_-_Edmund_Dulac_for_Andersen.jpg

YOU MAY ALSO LIKE

these Stelliform Press titles by Indigenous authors.

Lush worldbuilding and humor buoy this Hawaiian best-friends-save-the-world underwater fantasy novella.

This queer Tainofuturist science fiction novella links climate and colonization and underscores the importance of queer futures and Indigenous solidarity. A breathless read, packed with feeling.

EBOOKS ARE ALWAYS ON SALE AT WWW.STELLIFORM.PRESS

Earth-focused fiction. Stellar stories. Stelliform.press.

Stelliform Press is shaping conversations about our climate changed world and our place within it. We invite you to join the conversation by leaving a comment or review on your favorite social media platform. Find us on the web at www.stelliform.press and on Mastodon, Bluesky, Instagram, Facebook, and Threads @StelliformPress.